KARMA'S DOMAIN

Summer Spirit Series book 2

SAMANTHA JACOBEY

Lavish
Publishing LLC

First Edition

Summer Spirit Series, book 2

All Rights Reserved

Published in the United States by Lavish Publishing, LLC, Midland, Texas

Cover Design by: Victor R. Sosa

Cover Images: Canstock

Paperback Edition

ISBN: 978-1-64900-091-0

www.LavishPublishing.com

Contents

PART I
Karma's Minion

Prologue

"Yes, I know… It's ok, you don't need to come… No, we're fine, Bel; I'll let you know."

Charlie stood at his bedroom door, listening to his mother's conversation, or her half of it at least. *Aunt Belinda's worried*; about him or Beth, he couldn't be sure. Moving across the hall, he started the shower and dropped his boxers. Climbing beneath the cool spray, he sighed loudly as the water pummeled the top of his head. *Today's the day.*

The young man, barely twenty, tried not to think about what lay ahead, but his mother's twin sister wasn't the only one concerned about the future. Unable to keep the memory at bay, his mind drifted back to the morning seven months ago, when a pair of men had attempted to rob the patrons at a coffee shop where he sat eating breakfast. He had jumped one of them to stop the attack, and in a fit of rage had beaten the man to death in the process. *Or he died a few days later; either way.*

Shutting his eyes tightly, as if to block out the bloody scene, he could hear the muted screams and chaos that had surrounded him. He recalled the feel of the metal napkin holder in his hand, being crushed by the force as he applied it, and the sound of the bones being splintered in what once had been a human skull.

A few of the onlookers had stopped during the event and filmed the incident instead of running away, and his attorney had been given a copy of the video. He had watched it several times, and it had become ingrained in his mind forever.

"*That's not self-defense,*" he heard his lawyer, Ken Carter, say again.

"That's not self-defense," he repeated to himself as he leaned against the wall. Forcing his mind away from the painful realization that he was in fact a murderer, he thought of Clarisse instead. The tall blonde had been his guardian angel ever since he was a small boy, and they had finally met two summers ago; the summer that he had been hit by a car and died.

She had taken him in when he crossed into the other plane, and had been training him to be a Summer Angel, who would help humans avoid certain nasty events in their lives. His memory of that time should have been removed completely when Destiny returned him to the plane of the living, but he had regained a fair number of recollections and events from that time, particularly where the Dark Angel Gous was concerned.

Focusing on the girl, he pictured her standing on the beach in Miami, her long blond strands floating around her. She looked very similar to the Donna, the girl he had bought a ring for and had hoped to marry, but there were subtle differences that intrigued him; the deeper, crisper blue of her eyes... the paleness of her skin. Clarisse had been more like meeting a ghost, even though her flesh had been warm in his grasp. He sighed, recalling her slender fingers entwined with his as she magically transported them from one place to another.

"Baby, are you 'bout done in there?" his mother's bang on the door and sharp tone jerked him back to the shower.

"Yeah," he cut off the water, "I'll be right out."

"'K," she called more softly, "We don' wanna be late," she informed him.

"I know," he agreed, holding out his hand as the towel on the rack next to him floated up to meet his fingers. He had been practicing using his powers, even though his instincts had told him he shouldn't. *I can't help it,* he rationalized; *besides, I might need them someday, and that means I need to know how to use them well.*

ONE

All Rise

"WE'RE IN HERE," Ken Carter indicated the small room for Charlie and his mother. Stepping inside the eight by eight cubical, the pair took seats side by side and stared at the man across the table from them.

At twenty-eight, Ken might have been older than Charlie, but he had only been out of law school for a year. Beth had her doubts about his being able to defend her son adequately. She would have spent every dime she had to fund the cause, but in the end he wouldn't allow it; so the young hot shot with a brand new practice had been chosen for the task.

"Wha's wrong?" she demanded curtly, her heart racing as her hand squeezed Charlie's firmly.

"Relax, mom," the younger man implored. "Ken's got this," he shot his lawyer a quick grin.

Not looking at the couple, Ken shuffled a few papers and folders in his briefcase before opening one of the files onto the table. "We go before the judge today," he reminded them, "and we need to be sure we're on the same page. You have waived your right to a trial by your peers; a smart move, I can assure you."

"Yeah," Charlie agreed, having decided to plead guilty to involuntary manslaughter. "You're right, they wouldn't care why it happened after they saw that video," he cringed.

"Yes, an unfortunate piece of evidence. But now we get to present our case to the judge, and hope for leniency in your sentencing. However, the prosecution will undoubtedly show the clip, and you need to be prepared. Remember, no outbursts; I want you to appear calm," he cut his eyes over at Beth. "If your emotions get the better of you, keep it as simple and as contained as possible. That man had a mother, too. No matter what he did, she wants to see Charlie punished for taking his life."

"I understand," she sniffed, her bottom lip quivering.

Shaking his head, Ken addressed his client, "You, on the other hand, can feel free to dispense with a few quiet tears; remorse is a good thing, and it shows your heart is in the right place. When you are on the stand, remember to relax and take your time. The prosecution is going to hammer you, and you can't let them get to you; he'll want to display your temper, and you can't allow that to happen." Ken closed the folder and ran his hand through his sandy curls. "I'm sorry this case turned out like it did; I know I promised I could get you off, but when we got the video in discovery, I realized it wouldn't be easy to win; damn near impossible in fact."

"It's ok," Charlie forced a smile. "We picked you because o' your experience as a public defender. You've seen a lot o' cases; you know how juries are gonna see things, an' I appreciate your help. Maybe th' judge'll understand, and I won' serve much time."

Beth sobbed, and Charlie dropped her hand, laying the arm across her shoulders. "It's ok, mom. You know where this's going… we have to be strong; it'll be ok," he soothed.

"I know," she sat up straighter, adjusting her new blouse over her rounded form. "I'm gonna do a good job for you, son; I promise." Wiping at her damp cheeks with pudgy palms, she nodded at his attorney, "Anything else?"

"No, that's it; we go in and listen to the prosecutor, and then we present our side. The judge will call for a recess so he can consider the evidence, and either pass sentence later today or tomorrow," he stood. "Either way, we have to appear calm and ready for whatever he decides."

Getting to their feet, the trio made their way out into the sparsely furnished corridor. Standing next to one of the leather covered benches outside their courtroom, Charlie could see prosecutor Ted Taylor down the hall; a tall older man, with slicked back gray hair, and a black suit.

The deceased young man's mother stood by his side, her clothes pristine, and her shiny purse hanging from her arm. *Yup, she wants to see me locked away for a long time.* He knew the odds were good he would do a year in prison, but that was far better than the sentence he could have received if she had gotten her way, and Ken seemed to think that she would have.

The boy he had killed had no record, and the friend who had been with him had insisted they had done it as a stupid prank; poor judgement on their part. They had been smoking weed all night before going into the shop with the intention of scaring everyone, and he denied that they were actually going to rob them. Everyone believed Charlie was the one in the wrong. *Funny; it's hard to argue with a dead body and blood on my hands.*

The wide doors opened and the bailiff ushered them inside. Taking his seat behind the large wooden table, Charlie glanced up at Ken, who stood on his right while he pulled the files out of his black case and laid them on the table, along with a thin yellow notepad. Over his shoulder, his mother sat stiffly behind him, but he avoided looking at her for fear she would begin to cry in earnest. Beyond her, a few other people had filed in as well, and he felt mildly curious who else would be interested in the proceedings, but not enough to actually turn around to see.

Not looking at the prosecutor or his victim's mother, Charlie folded his hands onto the flat surface before him and toyed with his fingers.

A few minutes later, the bailiff called loudly, "All rise," and he quickly got to his feet, remembering to keep a straight face as he smoothed the front of his new suit. His heart pounded in his ears, so loud he could hardly hear the words as the judge read off the case information to the court reporter.

The prosecutor wasted no time, and almost immediately had a large screen lowered from the ceiling, where he displayed the video of Charlie bludgeoning the crazed young male, causing a stir in the vast seating area to his back. Watching himself sit on the man's chest, he recalled that Gous had more than likely sent the pair to attack him, but he had kept that piece of information to himself.

Only half listening to the proceedings, his mind wandered away as he considered the strange turn of events. As it were, he would go to prison, with a finite amount of time to be served. If he proclaimed that a Dark Angel had arranged the whole incident, he would likely end up in a mental hospital for who knows how long.

"Here, we see that he had to be pulled off the victim," the attorney pointed out the sequence of events. "Several of the onlookers helped to subdue him until the police arrived." His voice deep, heavy with condemnation, the dark suit fit him perfectly as Ted paced in the open area between the tables and the bench. "This is a demonstration of his character; one in a clear pattern of deviant behavior."

Opening a file, he presented a small stack of pages to the judge, "I have here sworn affidavits from ten students who attended high school with Mr. Phillips, each of them attesting to his dark temper and violent mood swings. There are also three teachers who agree with those assessments."

Instant recognition flashed in his mind, and Charlie knew who would make such claims. He'd had few friends in high school; with Brett Nelson there to bully him while leading the group of cool kids, his life had been difficult to endure. It had only been after his near death experience that he had changed, and he hoped that Ken could convince the judge of that when they got their turn.

Remembering to remain still, Charlie stared at a spot above the prosecutor as he paced, not daring to watch him directly. The nape of his neck burned, and he could feel the eyes of those behind him boring into the back of his head. Growing uneasy, he ran his fingers firmly over the singed spot. He cautiously shifted and glanced over his shoulder to find a young woman watching him intently. *Probably a reporter; or another of his family.*

The girl had auburn hair, swept up into a neat bun. Her makeup bright and easy to see on her dark flesh, her sparkling red lips matched the color of her suit. Crossing her legs, she shifted her gaze to the judge as he listened to the evidence, a small smile emerging when she noticed that Charlie had begun to stare in her direction.

Realizing he'd been caught, he adjusted himself so that the temptation to look at the red-headed beauty had been removed. This was neither the time nor place to flirt, even if the woman had seemed receptive to the idea. Refocused on the hearing, Charlie waited to be called to the stand. Upon hearing his name, he stood, steadying his nerves as he crossed the open floor and mounted the small platform calmly. Before taking the seat, he raised his right hand and swore that what he said would be the truth.

"Mr. Phillips, you were alone the morning you went into the café, were you not?" Ted Taylor dug in.

"Yes, sir," Charlie nodded slightly, his eyes darting to the rows of seats and the clear green eyes that focused on him.

"And why didn't your mother accompany you? The two of you were traveling together," his tone insinuated going alone had been an indicator of trouble.

"My mom was sleeping in," Charlie's voice wavered, then grew stronger, "I didn't want t' drag her out o' bed that early, so I went t' get some coffee and relax on my own." Swallowing, he glanced at the judge. He could read the name plate, *Judge Henry Arnold*, from that vantage point, and felt a chill run up his spine.

The prosecutor continued the interview, pushing at Charlie and demanding explanations for seemingly simple acts from his past; things that in retrospect did not speak well of his character. Doing his best to provide short, concise answers, he felt drawn to the woman he had never seen before, noticing that she no longer looked at him at all; *she thinks I'm lying. They all do,* he inwardly moaned.

Feeling sunk, he did his best to make it through the interrogation, until it finally came his attorney's turn to repair the damage. Going through the series of questions that they had rehearsed, Charlie relaxed, and even managed a smile from time to time, as he recalled how he had changed over the last year, and his own sheaf of supporters' statements were presented.

Allowed to return to his seat at the table when they were done, he stood and made his way across the front part of the courtroom. Squaring his shoulders and running his hands down the front of his suit, Charlie avoided looking at his mother. He had heard her sniffle several times during his testimony, and he could picture her bawling at any moment.

Instead, he glanced around at the stern faced group of onlookers, who numbered about a dozen now that he could see them all; he wondered again what they were all doing there. His eyes once again meeting those of the red-head as he reached his seat, her cold glare froze him on the spot, and he paused, unable to move.

"Charlie, sit down," Ken hissed, following the younger man's gaze and seeing what had distracted him. Once his client had complied, he continued, presenting the last of his evidence and praying it would be enough to sway the judge away from the maximum sentence.

TWO

Saved by the Belle

CHARLIE COULD FEEL his heart beating furiously inside his chest. *What did he just say?* The judge couldn't have meant that. *He can't possibly be ready to pass judgement; we just finished presenting the evidence!*

"Your honor, if I may," the young red-headed woman spoke from the gate that separated the audience from the bench area.

"Ms. Kapoor," Judge Arnold raised his hand, wafting her to step forward. Immediately, both attorneys leapt up to join them at the bench.

Their voices low, the girl spoke to the judge and then listened to the reply, followed by a mild flutter of discussion from each of the others before the man behind the bench waved them to their seats.

"On second thought, we will have a bit of a recess," he informed the courtroom. "We will reconvene after lunch, at two pm, and I will pass sentence at that time." Standing, the bailiff called for everyone to rise as he exited the room, with the fiery red bun following close behind.

As soon as they were gone, Ken exhaled a loud breath, then turned to inform his client and his mother, "I have to go to that meeting. You guys go have a nice lunch, and don't worry; I know it doesn't look like it, but I think things just took a turn in your favor." Gathering his things, he joined the prosecutor, and they made their way into the judge's chambers together, leaving Charlie and his mother staring at the other woman who had been watching the proceedings in surprise.

"Now what?" Bethany demanded angrily.

"Now we have lunch," Charlie darted through the short divider and grasped her arm, pushing her towards the exit and past those that still remained. As soon as he had steered her outside, the warm California sun beat down on the top of his head and he paused for an instant, thinking of Clarisse. "It could have been worse," he informed her as they made their way down the walk. "Let's not dwell on it and find a spot to get a good meal."

Choosing an open-air café, he selected a table along the edge so that the bright light shown on his arm and leg. Removing the stiff jacket, he hung it over the back of his chair and casually plopped down while wishing he were old enough to order a stiff drink.

"Watch it," his mother snapped angrily, "You're gonna wrinkle that thing, an' it was expensive."

"Peanuts," he shot back, cutting his eyes up from his menu to give her a small grin.

"Oh," she inhaled sharply, remembering their code word for when she was behaving negatively, "Sorry, baby. Mama's just anxious about all this," she waved her hand at nothing in particular.

"I know," he agreed, laying his brightly colored card on the table and pointing at his choice, "This looks really good. I think we should try it."

Stretching to see over the condiments in the center of table, she nodded, "Ok, I'll take one, but I don' know that I can eat."

"I know," he agreed, looking around for the waiter who had gone to get their drinks. "Relax, ok? The hard part's behind us; the judge has heard everything, and all we do now is find out what th' sentence is gonna be. Then I'm off for a bit, but I don' want you t' worry -"

"Not yet," she held up her hand to cut him off. "Don' say anything until we've heard the sentence."

Nodding a reluctant agreement, he scanned the street next to them, his mind drifting to the dream he had recently had; one from his time on the other side. He and Clarisse had been popping around the world, and had sat at a table much like that one, only it had been in New York and the day had not been nearly as cheerful.

"It's all gonna work out, mom," he reassured her absently. He wished that his best friend could be there to make sure of that, but he knew she was still in time out, where Keeper had placed her. At least he figured as much, since she had not contacted him to let him know any different. Of course, that meant the Dark Angel wasn't around either, so it could be considered a fair trade.

Enjoying the meal, the pair discussed his classes, which had ended before the holiday. "It sure felt weird, having Christmas here where it's not even cold," he chuckled. "I'm glad they're going to let me come back whenever I get out, so I won't lose my place."

"Yeah," she quickly agreed, "But I'm still hopin' you'll be able t' have those long distance classes like your advisor suggested."

Charlie nodded, glad she seemed calmer, "If I'm housed in the right prison, it'll happen, but if it don't, we'll manage." He knew dark times lay in his future, and the prospect of earning his degree while behind bars both gave him hope and tore him apart at the same time. However, her well-being had become his greatest fear, even if it wasn't the time to discuss it. "I'm glad I took this semester off, either way; I'll get back on track when I can," he consoled. Leaning back in his chair, he pushed his plate away to stretch. "Man, that was good stuff."

"Yeah," Beth agreed, swirling her unfinished portion around with her fork. She knew there were things they needed to talk about; important things, and time was running out. However, she couldn't bring herself to face them; soon their apartment would be empty. She still had her new job, and could support herself without dipping into the money they had saved after all their expenses from the move, so that wasn't the problem.

The problem would be having to let him go so soon after they had finally found peace between them. Putting her fork down, she wiped her lips and lay the linen napkin across the plate. She didn't dare speak the words, but she knew her life was about to change in less than an hour, and she would again lose someone very dear to her.

Paying their bill, the pair walked hand in hand towards the court-house. Their pace almost leisurely, Charlie wondered how his life might have been different if they had set aside their differences long ago. *She is my mother, after all.* Her attitude qualified as poor while he was growing up, but still, he could not blame her entirely for the rift that had formed between them.

Through the years, the boy had done things to irritate her, almost taking pleasure in seeing her face grow red when she went into one of her tirades; and she wasn't the only one. *I guess I really wasn't that great of a person; even if Brett picked on me, I didn't make friends because I didn't really want to.* He had reached the point of realizing he couldn't blame others for all the bad in his life.

And now Karma's come to get me, he chuckled, recalling that everyone gets what's coming to them in the end. The thought of Karma sent his mind leaping to Phillip Parson, the stranger who had hitched a ride with the pair when they were outside Phoenix. *The Forgotten Angel.*

Phil had warned Charlie to stay on Karma's good side; *"she's a real bitch,"* he had declared in parting. He had also warned him about telling his mother too much and poisoning her life. That's one piece of advice Charlie had taken to heart, and he had never said anything further to her about Clarisse, Gous, angels, or anything of the like.

Also, he had taken great care to ensure he never used his power in the presence of another person; period. People weren't supposed to see magic, but he wasn't taking any chances.

When everything turned out so badly, with Clarisse and Gous locked up by Keeper, he had hoped he would earn a few points on the positive side by living well and taking care of his mother. *I guess Karma's got a long memory,* he sighed to himself, reflecting on his current situation.

Making their way through security, they rode the elevator to the third floor, arriving with ten minutes to spare. "There you are!" Ken called as soon as they stepped out of the shiny metal doors. "Breaks over; the judge is ready to give his decision," he urged them towards the court-room, where the bailiff closed the doors behind them.

"What? He's early," Beth tried to argue, but found herself brushed aside when they reached the short wall and gate that divided the room.

Feeling flustered, Charlie's face took on a bright pink hue as he was ushered to his seat at the table in front. While shuffling down the aisle, he had seen that the number of observers had nearly doubled. His gaze briefly meeting that of Ms. Kapoor, his heart raced at her cool stare. *This is no time for pretty girls,* he grimaced, sliding into his chair only to stand again as instructed by the bailiff.

Glancing over his shoulder at the crowd behind him, Charlie longed to reach for his mother; to hold her hand and comfort her as judgment was passed. Resuming their seated positions, the room remained quiet as they waited for Judge Arnold to read his decision.

Looking over the top of his reading glasses, the court official shuffled the pages before him for a moment, then said in a stern voice, "Charles Phillips, please stand."

Obediently on his feet, with his attorney at his side, Charlie waited. His breath lightly passing over his lips, he silently begged, *dear God, just read the damn thing already.*

"Charles Andrew Phillips, you have entered a plea of guilty to involuntary manslaughter in the death of Fredrick Albert Shoemaker, in what can only be categorized as a form of vigilante justice. I am appalled at what I saw in the video that was taken of you committing an act that could easily have been deemed as murder," he growled, causing a whisper of *amen* to flutter through the crowd.

"However, you are not on trial here today," the judge bellowed. "Instead, you have accepted responsibility for this boy's death. Some, namely your attorney, Mr. Carter, contend that you aren't much more than a boy yourself, and although your actions were stupid to say the least, that you should be allowed to pay penance for your mistakes, and then to go on and live your life in peace."

A more disgruntled mummer rippled through the rows of observers, and the judge paused, giving them a stern stare before he continued to speak. "I realize that my decision will not be popular with everyone; rulings seldom are, as there are always two sides to every story. However, it is my decision that rather than have you sit on your rear in a prison, you will instead be remanded to the custody of a rehabilitation project for two years of community service."

The room erupted into a frenzy, and Charlie could see that the victim's mother was on her feet, screaming, "That's not fair!" from the corner of his eye. Swallowing hard and not daring to look away, he kept his gaze fixed firmly on the man behind the bench.

Applying his mallet to a small wooden block, the judge called for everyone to sit and be quiet. "I will clear this room," he shouted and waited for the racket to subside. When the viewers had taken their seats, he concluded, "This is no slap on the wrist that you have received. You will remain on the facility grounds for the duration of your sentence. You will only leave to conduct work to be determined by the facility management. You will be granted one two-hour visit by family members per month. You will be granted two hours of phone time per week; a privilege that can be revoked for non-cooperation with community directives. You will perform two hundred and fifty clock hours of community service, and attend another two hundred and fifty clock hours of therapy sessions as determined by your counselor."

Inhaling deeply, the judge paused, then said in a calmer tone, "If you fail to complete your time in either of those capacities, or if your counselor informs me that you are non-compliant in your sentence at any time, you will be remanded into the custody of the State of California for a term of five years in a penitentiary, without the possibility of parole."

Standing abruptly, the judge left his seat and headed for his chambers while the room once again echoed with angry voices.

THREE

Not Really Goodbye

"WHAT THE HELL DOES THAT MEAN?" Charlie exploded, still staring at the door the judge had used as an exit.

"It means, we worked out a deal," Ken grinned, shaking Charlie's hand.

"A deal?" the younger man's voice grew louder as he yanked his arm free. Glancing at his mother, he could see she appeared too stunned to speak. "Five years? That don' sound like a deal to me!"

"Relax, Charlie," Ken leaned closer, "You only do five years if you don't complete the community service. And the judge didn't really explain it very well, but you actually have two years to complete the program. If you work hard, you could actually go home in less."

"Go home in less," Charlie nodded his head around in an exaggerated fashion, "And what th' hell is mom supposed t' do while I'm gone? You said I would get a year, Ken!"

"I know what I said," the attorney straightened his tie, turning to watch as the last of the court observers were shown out of the room. Thankful for the silence around them, he exhaled loudly in frustration, "It's hard to tell what a judge is going to do some times. They get it in their head that they need to really punish people; you know, like a judge," he taunted.

"So that's what you guys worked out in your little meeting?" Charlie pulled off the stuffy jacket and tossed it over the table.

"Yes, more or less. When we got in the judge's chamber, he had already decided he was going to give you the five years. But, Ms. Kapoor wanted you for their new program; she says you'll be perfect," Ken smiled encouragingly.

Beth, who had been waiting for the right moment to jump into the conversation decided the time had come, "You mean that girl in th' red dress? She's the one runnin' th' community service?"

"Yes, Bethany," the attorney faced her to make another appeal. "I swear to you, this is a good thing. It's easy; it's safe. Not like prison, where bad things could have happened to Charlie, especially having to be there for five years."

"Uh-huh," she looked unconvinced, her hands on her hips.

Pushing her to understand, he continued, "And we can get his college to do online classes for him. Ms. Kapoor said the program is all about improving their lives and turning them around; getting an education is encouraged."

Pursing his lips, Charlie studied the man they had trusted, wondering if they had made a mistake. *Of course it's too late now,* he mentally conceded. "When do I go?" he demanded tartly.

"Tomorrow," Ken leaned his rear on their table and relaxed a bit. "Ms. Kapoor will pick you up at my office at eight-thirty, so you get to spend the evening with your mom. Pack everything you're going to need in a few suitcases or boxes, or whatever, but I wouldn't take too much."

"Everything I need," Charlie nodded again as if his head might roll off his shoulders at any moment, "For two whole years."

"Hey, don't think of it that way," Ken frowned, "You get to go home when you're done; so get in there, find out what you have to do, and don't let up until it's all finished."

Picking up his jacket, Charlie turned to Beth, looking down into her wide brown eyes. He could see the sadness, as well as how she fought the tears. She had taken the news better than he thought she would after the way she had carried on beforehand; *I guess it really is worse not knowing.*

"It'll be ok, baby," she leaned against him, pulling him into a firm squeeze. "The judge said I get t' visit once a month, an' that means you're gonna be close by. An' we get t' talk on th' phone every week, so this two years is gonna fly by!"

Her positive attitude sounded odd, and Charlie had his doubts, but the argument was moot. Guiding her towards the door, he at least hoped that the angry mob had moved on and they could exit the courthouse in peace. Finding the corridor outside empty, the pair made their way to the elevator and out of the building unscathed.

Arriving home that afternoon, their tiny apartment only served as a sad reminder of what lay ahead. Opening the front door, Charlie carried a couple of boxes they had picked up from the back of the grocery down the street under his arm. "I'm really not gonna take much," he informed his mother as he dropped them on the floor and went to search for the roll of tape in the junk drawer.

"Take what you need t' be comfortable," Beth replied sadly, moving to his bedroom door and switching on the light in an effort to brighten her mood. Starting with the dresser, she pulled out a few items and lay them on the bed. "I'm really gonna miss you," she sniffed when he joined her with the assembled boxes.

"I know," he set down the cartons and took her in his arms. "I'm really sad t' be goin', but we need t' get this behind us. I guess two years is damn sure better than five, so I'm gonna suck it up an' get this done. And Ken's right; it beats actual prison." Laying his head against the top of hers, he sighed. "This isn't really goodbye, mom. We're gonna keep in touch; I had an idea about that, too."

Pulling away, she stepped back and wiped away her tears, forcing a brave smile, "Ok, how're we gonna do it?"

"I've got my email, and you've got yours," he grinned. "We'll use that way, and if I'm allowed my Facebook, we can message each other, too. Save th' phone calls for really important stuff, where a message just won't do." Cocking his head, he silently wondered for a moment how they were going to prevent him from using his cell phone, but didn't bother to mention it; *I'm sure they've some way of controlling it, or they wouldn't have mentioned it.*

Nodding, Beth smiled up at him before she began opening more drawers to help him pack. "I think you should take a good variety o' clothes, an' all o' your socks an' underwear. Since we don' really know where you're goin', who knows what th' weather'll be like," she said more crisply to raise their spirits.

"True," he agreed, arranging the items into his cartons. "Are you gonna have enough money without my income while I'm gone?" he asked, realizing he needed to inform his boss at the shoe store that he would not be back, indefinitely. "I need to call the shop and tell them I quit," he mumbled aloud.

"I'll be fine, baby," she sniffed again, still smiling, "My job pays pretty decent, an' I should be able t' make it without dippin' into th' savin's; an' I'll even put some back in it if I can."

"Well, you let me know if that changes," he sighed, tossing a shirt onto the floor to start a *no* pile, "I'm not takin' all this stuff. I never wear some of it now, why would I wear it there?" he laughed.

"I'll donate them to goodwill if you don' wan'em anymore," she said as she sat another stack on the bed for him to sort through.

Together, they chose a location for all of his clothing, and put what he would be keeping into the boxes or back into a single drawer, leaving the rest of them and the closet empty. Using a couple of trash bags, he gathered up the donation pile for her and carried them down to his car, placing them in the back compartment and the boxes into the back seat.

The sun had begun to set, and he paused to stare across the road as it sank into the water. His view of it and the beach from their new home extraordinary, he muttered, *damn; I hate to leave this place.* It reminded him of Clarisse, the love of his life, and had become the first place he had ever really felt at home.

Trudging back inside, he shook the key fob at her and grinned deviously, "Take good care o' my baby while I'm gone."

"Oh, your gonna trust me with your car?" she shot back while starting dinner.

"Yeah, I'm not gonna need it, apparently. But I would like a ride t' Ken's office before you go in t' work," he informed her as he dialed his own employer to resign.

Not bothering to reply, Beth turned her back and fidgeted with the meal, hiding her tears as they dripping onto her blouse. Letting him go would be hard enough without making a big deal about it, after all.

FOUR

Highway to Nowhere

"GOOD MORNING, CHARLIE," Ken called, taking the box from him when he lifted it out of the back seat. "Here, let me get that, and you can get the other one. Good morning, Beth," he nodded across the roof as she exited the vehicle.

Carrying his only suitcase, Bethany followed as the men took the boxes inside. Grabbing her son quickly after placing the bag onto a lobby chair, she hugged him tight. "I'll talk to you soon, baby," she informed him before spinning on her heel and fleeing the room.

"Wow, that was quick," Ken observed her through the front glass as she climbed into the car and sped away.

"Yeah, she's upset. I guess that's what you could call her Band Aid method to avoiding issues; rip it an' run," the younger man laughed, then offered his hand. "I didn' thank you yesterday for all that you've done. It could've ended a lot worse; I'm sorry I yelled at you about it."

"Hey, don't mention it," Ken gave the appendage a few pumps before indicating a chair. "I've got some work to do, but I'll be in my office if you need me, and help yourself to some of the coffee if you like, while you wait."

"Thanks," Charlie grinned, reaching for a cup as his attorney closed the door to the next room behind him. Smiling at the young girl behind her desk, he took a seat to wait for Ms. Kapoor. *That's an interesting name,* he thought to himself as he considered it.

His mind turning over what he knew about the young woman with the fiery-redish hair, he recalled her deeply colored skin. She had appeared tall standing at the front of the courtroom when they were huddled up for her confab with the judge, but since she had on a pair of spiked stilettos, it had masked her true height, he felt certain.

A few minutes later, the woman in question opened the door briskly, and announced, "Well, you're here and ready. That's good. My car is parked right outside."

Whisking herself back out without so much as offering to help, Charlie stared after her for a moment with a wide open jaw. Snapping it shut, he hoisted the largest of the boxes and carried it outside, where Ms. Kapoor stood next to a bright red Ferrari Spider. "You expect all my stuff to fit in *that?*" he demanded curtly, already unimpressed by his more or less new boss and her expensive ride.

"Yup," she punched a button on her fob and the front popped open, exposing the tiny cargo area. Leaning against the passenger window, she stared at her phone while he carried his box over and dropped it into the shallow trunk.

Staring at the parcel with wide eyes, it fitted snugly into the small space, but had cleared on all sides. Shrugging, he stomped back inside, bringing out the second box, with the suitcase slung over his shoulder.

Plopping the second box on top of the first, he squeezed the suitcase into the open area left between them and right hand wall. *A perfect fit, if it closes,* he conceded as he reached for the cover and slammed it down.

Looking up at him, the woman's satin red lips curved into a smile, "Would you like the top up or down?" She wore a red pantsuit, her white top emphasizing her cleavage, and her auburn hair hung over her shoulders and cascaded down her back in a riot of waves.

"I, uh," he stammered, drawn in by the deepest brown eyes he had ever seen; *I could've sworn her eyes were green yesterday.* "I don't care, either way," he managed a grin.

"Good," she gathered her shiny locks, twisting them up into a bun and applying a golden clip to hold them into place. Strutting round the car in her high-heeled, red leather boots, she slunk down into the driver's seat and hit a button inside. In an instant, the roof popped up and folded over, fitting nicely into the storage area behind the seats. "Hop in, Charlie."

Grunting, he opened the door and melted into the passenger seat. As they pulled easily out onto the highway a few minutes later, he watched the woman next to him in utter awe. *Who the hell is this girl?*

Deciding to wait to play twenty questions, he stared out the front glass, only daring periodic glances in her direction. Her eyes hidden behind her shades, he wondered how he could have missed their almost ebony shade; *but, she wasn't right in front of me, either,* he decided.

As they took the 10 out of L.A. and headed towards Arizona, he shouted with a frown, "Where are we going?"

Shooting him a quick smirk, she smoothed a few loose strands of hair and called back, "We're going to our community center; it's a little off the beaten path." Spying a station ahead, she pulled in and put up the top, commenting off handedly, "That should make talking easier. We need to go over the rules before we get there."

Stepping out, she opened the fuel tank access, "Would you mind filling it up while I visit the ladies' room?" Not waiting for his reply, she sauntered inside and paused at the counter to hand the attendant a few folded bills before disappearing out of sight.

"Jeez," he muttered under his breath, further annoyed by her attitude towards him. Not really seeing another option, he then climbed out and did as she had requested. While he topped off the tank, she returned and handed him a bottled beverage before sliding back behind the wheel.

Staring at the container, he grimaced at the Dr. Pepper; at one time, it had been his favorite carbonated drink. The recollection of that fact made the hair on his neck prickle, but he couldn't exactly pinpoint why. Shutting the small door, he opened his and dropped his soda on the seat, "I need to take a leak, too," he informed her before slamming it shut and heading inside, whether she liked it or not.

The more time he spent in the company of *Ms. Kapoor*, the less he liked it. She appeared aloof, almost snooty, with a *holier-than-thou* air about her. Taking care of business and giving his hands a quick wash, he marched back to the car with a prepared list of questions.

Closing the door and fastening his seatbelt, he opened fire, "Ok, so who the hell are you?"

Smiling beneath her shades, she eased the car out onto the highway before she replied. "My name is Karma Kapoor, and I'm your new counselor. I run a small outreach program that helps troubled individuals find their way."

Again, the hair on his neck bristled, and he could feel his breathing growing shallow in excitement. "That's a pretty unusual name," he chose his words carefully. "So, do I call you Karma, or is it always Ms. Kapoor?"

"Karma will suffice," she flicked her gaze over at him briefly. "We're going to be together for a long time, Charlie."

"Two years isn't that long," he turned to look away, giving the side of the road out his window a long gaze. "And where exactly is this place we're going?"

"We have an out-of-the-way location," she supplied. "I've found that people in your situation tend to do better when they're not distracted by too much around them."

"I see," he rolled his tongue against his cheek for a moment. "So, how many people are out here at your little rehab center?"

"Rehab center," she repeated softly, "That's an interesting name for it. Accurate in a way, I guess. We currently have eight at our facility, which we affectionately call Purgatory."

"Purgatory?" his voice squeaked as he swung around to glare at her profile. "Why the hell would you call it that?"

"Because it's not really prison, but it's not home, either. It's not exactly a half-way house, although the idea is the same," she whipped into the left hand lane to pass a slower car smoothly, then eased back over in front of them. "You can relax, Charlie. I'm not going to hurt you. There's nothing sinister about Purgatory; it's just a place between worlds, where you can get your bearings. And we only have a few rules. There's no outside access except during designated hours. No one comes to visit, and no one leaves the compound without my permission. And finally, and this is the most important, Charlie; everyone here is respected. Failure to comply has severe consequences, and you don't really want to find out about those."

Grinding his teeth, Charlie's mind raced. He'd seen too many weird things in his life to not be on edge at that moment. *Karma; there's a coincidence for you.* And Purgatory? The phrase *a place between worlds* hadn't escaped him, either. Of course, the smart move would be to have a little patience, rather than demanding explanations. *If she doesn't know that I suspect, I'll get a lot more answers through observation.*

Keeping her eyes on the road, Karma steered them across the state line, finally taking a left onto a smaller road well before they got to Phoenix. The young man next to her seemed out of sorts, but had fallen into silence, and that was fine with her; he would find out all he needed to know as soon as they reached her little compound in the middle of nowhere.

FIVE

Bad Penny

CHARLIE STARED at the soft brown earth flying past his window, picking up on cracked and crusted spots here and there. The narrow road they had taken hardly qualified as more than a path, but with open dirt on either side, it was hard to say that it mattered. In the distance, a green patch loomed ahead of them, giving him an ominous feeling in his gut. *Purgatory, but like the Garden of Eden?*

As the area grew closer, he recognized a few trees, each standing like a giant, fluffy corner post to a large gray structure filled with glass windows. Emitting a small shudder when they pulled up in front of the massive estate, he reached for the handle and climbed out onto the firm ground of the driveway.

"Nice place," he remarked casually.

"Thanks," she grinned at his nonchalance. "Come on inside, and we'll get your stuff out of the boot after your tour."

The stone path that led to the double front door was flanked on both sides by green grass. Well-manicured, the lawn seemed out of place surrounded by a scorching desert, and two large rose bushes hugged the structure on either side. "How do you get it to grow?" he asked absently, pausing at the base of the single step.

"We have an underground water source," she supplied easily,

pointing at the pair of windmills off to the side of the house, between it and the barn. "This used to be a giant lake, but it moved underground centuries ago; we tapped into it." She opened the door and indicated for him to follow.

Inside, her boots clicked loudly on the wooden floor. From the outside, the place had appeared almost shabby, but inside, everything held a crisp, bright feel, despite the tinted glass. The stuffed couches in the sitting room to the left of the entrance filled in the space, forming a V-shape that looked out through the glass walls.

"Wow, this place is nice," he followed her into the sitting room.

"Of course," she indicated the plants that lined the entire glass barrier. "We call this the atrium and we have a rotating schedule for watering the plants. I'll show you where to find the duty board, and you'll want to be sure you don't forget when it's your turn. I get really cranky when my plants start turning brown," she grinned, but the effect gave him an odd twist in his gut.

"Ok," he nodded, his eyes taking in the rest of the room anxiously. Something about her did anything but put him at ease.

Moving to the corner, where the two glass walls met, he placed his hand against the glass for a moment, then withdrew it and sauntered along the far wall to where the next room began, indicated by the change in the flooring. A giant pair of tables sat in the center of it, each with eight chairs around and tile beneath them.

"You said there were only eight of us," he indicated the arrangement.

"Well, there are at the moment, but we are equipped to handle twice that number," she followed him into the dining space. "This way to the kitchen," she indicated across the bar.

Trailing along after her, he observed more potted plants along the base of the glass exterior, only this time they were cacti, which would require a minimum amount of care. Walking through the kitchen, he noted that it had solid walls on three sides, and that a staircase to the right went both down and up. "You have a basement?"

"Yes, that's the work area. We have a gym, and everyone has a cubical for their computer. You will be assigned one, and be allowed access for two hours per day, and internet access one day per week, which is part of what we call your 'phone time', so use it wisely."

"Ah," he hoped he appeared calm at the realization they had thought of everything, and there would be no stolen chats with his mother. "You know, you said this isn't a prison, but it's starting to look an awful lot like one," he observed.

"Well, give it time," she breathed airily with a smile that made his skin crawl.

"Karma," a male voice called from the stairs as a muscular man with coal black hair descended them. "Oh good, your back," he continued when he had reached the bottom. "We have a problem with Lorren -"

She cut him off with a wave of her hand, "Not now, Phil. I'm showing our newest guest around," she indicated the newcomer with an open palm.

"Phil?" Charlie stared at him with obvious surprise. "Phil Parson?" he demanded a little more forcefully. His opinion of Purgatory took a nose dive with the appearance of the bad penny that indicated trouble loomed in his future. *Maybe prison wouldn't be so bad after all.*

"Ah, you two are acquainted; lovely," Karma spun around and headed down the stairs, "Take over the tour, would you, hun? I'll be in my office when you're done," she called as her bun disappeared out of sight.

Letting her go, Charlie addressed the man he had met the last time he was in Arizona, "Care t' tell me wha's going on here?"

"What's going on?" Phillip laughed, indicating for him to follow him up the stairs, to the second level, "You didn't listen, that's what's going on."

"I did to listen," Charlie hissed at his back, "You said not t' poison my mother's life and I did exactly that. She doesn't know anything about… anything."

"Yeah, but you didn't listen to a damn thing I said about Karma, now did you?" Phil stopped at the first door on the right of the long hallway that divided the upper floor in half. "This is your room," he stepped inside. "I'm at the other end of the hall, and we each have one roommate, for now at least. His is that bunk," he indicated the lower bed on the right hand wall.

Pausing in the entrance, Charlie could see that it opened in the center of the wall that separated the room from the hall; *symmetrical.* He had noticed it downstairs, but it didn't really stick out until he stood there looking at another room where everything seemed to have a mirror; two sets of bunks, two sets of lockers, two chairs by the window, each on opposite sides of the room. "Is the whole house like this?" he asked, moving to the wall of glass that made up the exterior wall.

"Like what?" Phillip demanded tartly.

"I dunno; balanced," Charlie indicated the two chairs absently. "In the atrium, there were two couches, one for each window. In the dining area, two tables. There were even two sinks in the kitchen."

"Hadn't noticed," Phil lied flatly, turning around and strutting out. "Welcome home, Charlie."

The younger man remained behind, taking the time to open a few drawers and cabinets in the storage units. Finding most to be empty, he mentally staked out which would stow his gear, and decided to take the other lower bunk on the opposite side of the room.

Once he had worked out his accommodations, he returned to the hall, where in fact the pairing pattern stood out more than ever; each door had a twin, one on each side of the hall, and an identical staircase went down on the far end.

Deciding to check it out, he peeked into the rooms as he passed. He discovered that the next pair, center of house, were a pair of large bath-rooms; each complete with two toilet stalls each along the left walls, identical storage units mounted on the back wall, and a pair of shower stalls on the right. *Looks like the dorms back in Austin,* he noted.

Descending via the far staircase, he located Phil on the lower level. "I thought you were giving me a tour," he didn't bother to hide his anger at the older man.

"Yeah," Phil smacked his lips, indicating the wall behind them, "That door takes you back out to the foyer, and you came in through the atrium on the other side. This is the great room; as you can see, it spans this whole side of the house."

Indeed a great room, it consisted of two large clusters of seating area, with couches that faced one another, and two chairs sitting side by side between them on the interior end. The second seating area mirrored the first, which by now had become expected.

"What's with all the windows?" Charlie indicated the latest glass wall.

Phillip laughed, his tone cynical, "That's our power supply."

Raising his eyebrows at him, Charlie had had just about enough of his attitude. "Ok, let's cut through the bullshit, shall we? You and I both know who the other is. You're an empath, an' I move shit," he slid the coffee table before them over a few feet with a wave of his hand for effect. "So how about you actually tell me what the hell is going on here."

"Not a chance," Phil sneered, turning to walk away. "Stay out of the barn; you only get in there if Karma invites you, and put that table back. She tends to freak out when things are out of place."

Staring at the balding back of his head as it disappeared down the second set of stairs to the basement, Charlie fumed. "Invited," he muttered, spinning on his heel and marching through the archway to the foyer. Slamming the front door behind him, he strutted down the path, realizing when he reached the car that he had no way to open it.

Closing his eyes, he dropped his head back and allowed the evening sun to cascade onto his face and neck. "Jesus, what the hell am I doing here?" he breathed aloud.

"It's ok, you can do it," a small voice called from behind him.

Righting his head, he swung around to face a young girl, five foot at best, with dark black hair and sullen brown eyes. Dressed in black jeans and an equally dark tee, a spiked leather collar around her neck gave him an uneasy feeling in the pit of his gut; *what, does she think she's a dog?*

"I'm not a dog," she shot back angrily, a tear instantly forming and spilling over onto her flushed cheek.

His mouth falling open, he gasped, "Did I say that out loud?"

"No," she snapped, "You didn't have to. I'm a telepath; I can hear you," she paused, *and speak to you*, her voice echoed inside his thoughts.

"Holy shit!" he gasped, thinking to himself, *I'm losing my damned mind!*

"No, Charlie," she smiled, taking a step closer to him. "It's my gift; my talent. I'm a telepath, and you're," she hesitated, but only for an instant, "Telekinetic."

The wheels turning, a cold chill worked its way up his spine, despite the heat of the desert sun. "Oh my God," the realization of his whereabouts poured over him, "Purgatory is a prison for the Forgotten Angels." He knew he had to get the hell out of there, and the sooner the better.

SIX

What Karma Can Do

LORREN STARED at him in surprise, "This isn't a prison; not really," she took another step closer, "You can open the car if you want. It's ok, I know about your gift."

Glancing at the flashy red vehicle that had brought him there, he considered his options. Deciding to remove his belongings, he released the latch after a moment of concentration and lifted the lid to reveal the empty compartment.

"I already got those for you, mate," a deep male voice informed him.

"Kari," Lorren smiled, a light flush coloring her cheeks. "This is Charlie,"

"Hullo, Charlie," the young man spoke again, his accent hard to miss as he offered his hand.

"You're from Australia, or England, or someplace like that," Charlie grinned, despite his recent revelations.

"I am from Australia," his new friend smiled widely. His dark ebony skin gave his teeth a vivid white sheen, and he placed his hand flat on his chest as he introduced himself. "I am Kari, which means smoke." When he nodded his head, his thick braids of coarse black hair shifted in clumps. Holding his hand out to indicate the missing baggage, he wafted it towards the house, "I have transported your belongings to our room."

"Our room," Charlie shifted slightly, "You're my roommate!"

"Yes, roommate," Kari nodded his agreement. "Come; let us have dinner and rejoice in the gathering."

Perplexed, Charlie followed the pair into the house, noting that the girl appeared quite smitten with the young man who bunked in his quarters. "How long have you guys been here?" he asked when they had made it inside.

Opening cabinets, Lorren bit her bottom lip for a moment, furtively glancing at Kari. Together, they produced hamburger meat, noodles, and vegetables for a salad once the sauce had begun to simmer and the water to boil. Showing Charlie where to find the plates and flatware, the girl informed him, "It's just us tonight; the three of us, Karma and Phil. Everyone else is away on business."

Counting out the plates and silverware, Charlie set one of the tables for the group to share the meal they had prepared. He felt angry at being tricked into coming there, but after having met some of the other residents, a sense of curiosity emerged. *I did want to find the Forgotten Angels, after all,* he rationalized; *and here Karma has pulled me into their midst.* Could he learn about them before he made his escape?

"You said this isn't a prison," he spoke to the girl softly when his chore had been completed. Glancing around anxiously, he could feel the tension radiating from the pair of them, "So why are you afraid to talk to me about it?"

Shaking her head, Lorren stirred the pot of long noodles, "It's not that I'm afraid. I've been here since I was a little girl. Karma brought me here after I drowned."

"You died," Charlie gasped, leaning in closer. "What about you?" he shifted his gaze to Kari. The other man only blinked at him a few times, so he pushed, "Look, I got hit by a car, two summers ago. I've seen the other plane, and I remember a lot about what's over there."

"That's impossible," Kari countered evenly.

"It's not," Charlie insisted, standing up straighter, "There's Dark Angels, that are like demons, and Summer Angels that look out for people. And these two great beings that are in charge of them, called Destiny and Fate -"

"That's enough!" Karma interrupted him sharply.

Turning to face her, his heart pounded. "Come on, you brought me here. Why?" A mixture of anger and fear roiled inside his gut, and he paused to see what she would do. *She can hear your thoughts,* Lorren's voice whispered in his head. Glancing at her, he knew that Karma had heard her speak to him, and that nothing inside of him was private.

Pulling himself up to his full height, he nodded at the woman of the house, "All right. I see how it is. Well, if you won't tell me, then there's no reason for me to stay here," he declared as he marched towards the front door.

"You can't leave," Karma announced loudly, taking her seat at the head of the table.

"Oh, I can leave," he assured her, not even breaking his stride.

"No; I'll call the judge, and you'll be in prison before the weekend," she threatened.

"So what," he spun around, "I'm not scared of prison. I've got powers, remember? Anyone who touches me is a bug that I can crush beneath my fist!" He ran his fingers through his brown waves, unsure why he would say such a thing.

"Good," Karma smiled, serving her plate from the pot that had been placed in the center of the flat surface before her. "You have realized your potential." The chair next to her scooted out from the table, seemingly on its own. "Come and eat, Charlie. I know you're hungry; we haven't eaten all day."

Refusing to comply, he inhaled deep breaths, pushing them out through his nostrils and causing them to flare. Watching while the pair who had prepared the meal joined her, he glanced around, "Where's Phil?"

"Oh, I'm sure he's sulking around here somewhere," Karma sighed. "Come on, hun; dinner will be cold before you can enjoy it."

At that moment, the door that exited the kitchen from the rear opened and Phil entered with a disgruntled expression on his face. "Did you save me any?" he demanded curtly before preparing his plate.

"There's always plenty," Karma grinned at his displeasure, then gave Charlie a long stare.

"I want answers," he insisted, watching the four of them enjoying their dinner as if nothing were wrong with anything that had happened.

"Yes, Charlie," Karma twirled her fork for a moment, "You always do, right? Have some patience. There is much that I can give you, if you only give me the chance."

Angrily stomping forward, Charlie snatched up his plate and filled it with slippery noodles. Spooning the bright red meat sauce over it, he retrieved his glass of tea from the counter in the kitchen and plunked down onto the chair, scooting it up to the table noisily. "I think you're a real bitch," he hissed at her, noticing that Phil paled three shades when he did it. The other two members of their party stopped moving and only stared for a moment before resuming their consumption.

Not giving him a reply, Karma cleaned her plate in silence, and no one dared to say anything before she had addressed the issue. Insubordination was not tolerated at Purgatory, and the sooner the new guy learned that, the better.

When she had finished, she lay her fork across the plate and placed her elbows on the table on either side of it. Folding her hands together, she leaned her chin on them and smiled at him. "Charlie, I realize that this has been difficult for you," the softness of her tone startled everyone. Sensing their surprise, she grinned even wider, "Let's play a little game, shall we?"

An uneasy squirm seemed to settle over the entire gathering at once, and each of them shifted and stretched anxiously. "I don' really like games," Charlie informed her bluntly.

"That's ok, hun," she agreed, "The others can play, and you can take a turn at the end. Right now," she raised her glass of wine as a toast to Kari, "Tell our new guest why you stay here. What is it that Karma has done for you," she spoke of herself in the third person, causing Charlie to smirk at his lap before he could hide it.

"Karma is a great warrior; the bringer of justice," Kari raised his own glass to her. "She has given me purpose in this world."

"Hear hear," Karma raised her goblet again. "What about you, Lorren. What has Karma provided for you?"

Cutting her eyes around at the group, one by one, the girl faltered before she replied, "Karma has given me a home. A place that I am accepted and I'm not afraid of my secret gift."

"Yes, and you will always be welcome here," their benefactor nodded at her. Giving Phil a long glare, she appeared to be considering whether or not to include him in the discussion, but he blurted a reply before she had officially asked.

"You're right, Charlie; Karma's a real bitch, and I warned you about that."

Stunned, Karma's eyes grew wide before she narrowed them into slits. "Phillip Parson, you know why you're here, and I won't tolerate that attitude. You should leave the table at once, before you get yourself into trouble."

"Gladly," he pushed his chair back and got to his feet. Taking the stairs with loud stomps, he eagerly left them to their pointless discussion.

"Please, forgive our disgruntled friend," Karma smiled at Charlie. "He's often in a foul mood; a side effect of his talent, I suppose." She took a sip from her glass, then placed it back on the table, "So, Charlie; what is it that you would like to have most?"

Her eyes twinkled when she stared at him, and he could almost see the dark chocolate color fading, and a soft green taking its place. Mesmerized by the beauty of the transition, he swallowed visibly, but said nothing.

"Come on, sweetheart. I know there is something that human heart of yours desires."

"My human heart," he repeated absently. Shaking himself free of his trance like state, he thought of Clarisse. He didn't say a word. He didn't have to; Karma knew what he wanted, even before he had formed the thought.

"I can get her for you," she whispered. He sucked his lips in, chewing the bottom one slightly, and she pushed, "I see what's in your heart, Charlie. I know that you loved her with all of your being."

Adjusting her glass on the table, she stood, her elegant red gown a robe that flowed around as she moved behind him, placing her hands on his shoulders to grasp him firmly. "I know what it's like to be separated from the thing that matters most. It is an unbearable pain," she paused, his thoughts turning to his mother. "Ah, you are concerned for her as well."

"Stop it," Charlie demanded, pushing her away from him as he got to his feet. "I don' know what game you're playin', but I don' want anything t' do with it!"

Her laugh a deep rumble, her eyes glowed a bright green, "Yes, Charlie, you want so badly for things to be the way they were; when the world was right and you had no knowledge of the truth. You are wise beyond your years, and you know the dangers that it can bring. Go to sleep my child," she wafted her hand at the stairs, "Rest your body and your mind, and we will speak again when you are fresh."

In an instant, she disappeared, leaving the three remaining in the room. Charlie looked down at the remains of the meal, stunned to see the plates and flatware vanish before his eyes as well. Walking over to the kitchen, Lorren touched a device, pushing a few buttons, and he could hear the sound of a dishwasher kicking on. "How...?" his eyes darted between the pair.

Giving each other a knowing stare, Lorren smiled, her grin devious as she revealed nothing. Instead, Kari stood, shrugging as he admitted, "I'm a transporter, mate. I move objects from one place to another."

"No shit," Charlie gasped, his understanding of the world changed once again. Staring through the clear glass that made up one wall of the dining area, he could see that the sun had set outside. Instinctively, he knew that the heat of the day would be replaced by the cool air of the evening. Thinking of the barn, he wondered if that's where Karma had gone, and what could be so special in there that he would have to be invited to see it.

SEVEN

The Real Deal

THE FIRST LIGHT of day glinted off the window when Charlie awoke. Across the floor, his roommate lay on his side, staring at him when he looked. "Good morning," he muttered, hoping to keep things civil in this new place that had only barely made sense.

"Good morning," Kari grinned, showing his beautiful white teeth. "You rested well?"

"Yeah," Charlie swung his legs over the side of the bunk, his eyes landing on the empty boxes that sat in the floor. They had been waiting for him when he arrived in his room the night before, just as Kari had promised, and he had unpacked them to calm his nerves before going to bed. Putting his items in the drawers that he had chosen had felt odd, and he now remained almost numb with the fear in his gut that he would never have his old life again.

Picking out a tee-shirt and jeans, he realized that Lorren or even Karma could be listening to his thoughts. Deciding it didn't matter, he turned the events of the last two days over in his mind, starting with the courtroom and how he had ended up in her custody. Almost immediately, the questions began to form; *I'm gonna have to talk to her, whether I like it or not.* He needed knowledge if he hoped to escape.

Donning a pale blue shirt and dark denim pants, Charlie shoved his feet into his sneakers and sighed. Glancing up, the bed across from him was empty, the room was empty, and Kari had left without saying a word. *I wonder if a person counts as an object.* He had never attempted to use his power on a person directly, and the idea of it made him cringe.

Down stairs, a feast awaited him, with each of the twin tables lined with everything a person could want for breakfast, including his favorite, fresh French toast and sweet syrup. Choosing a cup, he helped himself to the coffee while looking around and wondering where everyone else was.

"They've already eaten," Karma informed him, entering from the basement stairs.

"Ah," he said aloud, "You know it's rude to read another person's thoughts."

"Oh, Charlie," her laughter tinkled. Moving into the room, she wore a red tank top and knee length shorts, a nice change from her typically stiff choices. "Come and sit with me," she indicated a chair.

"Hmm," the young man grunted, glancing around again as he placed his mug on the table and began filling a plate. "So, tell me about those power windows," he indicated the panes of glass, having chosen something simple to begin his interrogation. "Are they magic?"

"No, they're not," she put her hands behind her back and pushed up onto her toes, then rocked back onto her flat feet; she had lost a few inches in the sneakers. "They're solar; they have all the workings inside of them and gather energy for the house; like a panel, only pretty."

Charlie's mind instantly flashed Clarisse standing on the beach and warming herself in the sun; recharging her power with its rays. "I see," he agreed, having never heard of such a thing.

"You are such a smart man," Karma praised, taking a plate of her own and adding a few items. Scooting into the seat across from him, the pair ate without another word passing between them, until they had finished. When their plates were clean, the entire service disappeared, and the room appeared spotless, as if it hadn't been used at all.

"Tha's a neat trick you have there," Charlie pointed at her and smiled. "I'm jealous, a bit."

"You have your talents," Karma countered, leaning back and crossing her right leg over the left.

"Yeah," he agreed, looking around him, "But it's not nearly as impressive as yours," he grinned at her. "So; care to fill me in on exactly what I'm doing here?"

"With pleasure," and an instant later, the pair stood on a beach, with the sun rising behind them and clear blue water before them.

Charlie instinctively knew they were on the west coast, and that his mother was not far off, in their little apartment. "Why have you done this?" he asked quietly.

"I had to," she informed him bluntly. "Charlie, you are a very special young man. And don't worry about your mom. You did well, hiding your secrets from her. I had feared that I would have to punish you; that you would bring it upon yourself, but you didn't."

"By revealing things t' her; poisoning her life."

"Exactly. It's my job to see that people get what they deserve, and it would have killed me to have been forced to destroy you," she paused, rubbing her hands together anxiously, "But I take my job very seriously. That's why only the worthy serve me in my house."

The wind rustling his hair, Charlie watched the waves roll up onto the shore, then slip back out into the ocean. "Tell me about Clarisse," he finally said quietly. "How are you gonna get her for me? We both know that Keeper has her locked away somewhere."

"Yes, but don't worry about that," Karma smiled at him. Her deep brown flesh shone warmly beneath the morning sun, the muscles in her arms exposed with her choice of top for the day. Offering him her hand, she continued, "I'll get her for you when the time comes; when you're ready."

Charlie placed his palm in hers, noting the warmth when their skin met, and in an instant they were swept across the world, and stood in an unfamiliar place. Before them, a group of teenagers were talking, laughing loudly a few times in the process.

Watching the group, who were sitting on benches and at tables in a courtyard, he recognized the location to be a school. Their banter appeared friendly, but he soon realized that one of the boys was being taunted, and the laughter at his expense. "Why are we here?" he turned to the woman next to him, briefly wondering if the group were aware of their presence.

"Just a quick lesson, that's all," she smiled, "And no, they don't see us. Or they are ignoring us, I guess would be more precise," she supplied, a smile curving her lips. "A few weeks ago, that boy lived in another town. He was forced to move here when his father changed jobs."

"Ok, so why are the other kids picking on him," Charlie squirmed, a bit disturbed by the memories the scene reflected in his past.

"Because, in his previous school, he was the bully," her grin twisted and became sinister. "Everyone gets what's coming to them, Charlie. Turnabout is fair play, and I see to it that everyone gets what they deserve."

A commotion ensued, as two of the boys dragged the newcomer off his seat, and then threw him to the ground. One holding him down, the other punched him repeatedly until blood covered his face and a small amount dotted the ground. Releasing him, the pair stood and walked away, the rest of the group following as a bell rang loudly inside the building behind them.

A feeling of de ja vu swept over him, and Charlie looked around anxiously, as if he were in a dream; one of the dreams he sometimes had about Clarisse. Seeing nothing out of place, he waited, turning to look at the woman next to him expectantly. When the boy rolled over and got to his feet, stumbling to collect his things and head inside, he demanded, "You're not even gonna help that kid?"

"I did help him," she grinned, and he could see the satisfaction on her face, "I saw to it that he got exactly what he deserved. This isn't the other plane, Charlie. This is the real world. My world. There are no angels here; no clients to be served. I deal in justice, plain and simple."

An instant later, they stood in the dining area in Purgatory. Staring at the cacti that lined the transparent wall, he sighed loudly, aware that she knew all that he knew, and she wasn't fooled by his attempt to garner information from her.

"Ok, let's get to it. I want to know everything," with his head down-turned, he cut his eyes up at her to make his demand.

"Sure, Charlie," her glossy red lips curled into a smile. Indicating for him to follow with her long fingers, she turned and walked to the front door.

Outside, Charlie observed the grass on either side of the path. His eyes drawn to the rose bushes, he again noted that there were two on each side; a pair standing side by side. "Why are there two of every-thing?" he demanded as they walked towards the barn.

"Because that is the way of nature," she supplied easily. "Do you not have two eyes? Two ears? Everything must have its equal; its balancing partner. A yin for a yang…" her voice trailed away as they reached the structure. Pausing in front of the massive doors, she waved her hand before them, and they parted.

The entrance swinging wide, the cool air hit him as he followed the mistress of the property inside. His eyes adjusting to the darkness of the room, the large panels closed behind them, and he realized that it wasn't a barn at all. "What is this place?" he breathed.

"This is my haven; the closest thing to home that I have on this plan-et," she twirled slowly in the middle of the floor. Surrounding them, the walls of the one massive room were lined with oversized couches, chairs and beanbags. Oddly, they also held draperies that covered non existent windows judging from the plain walls he had seen outside. Taking it all in, he also noted a large bed stood in one corner, with at least a dozen fluffy pillows calling to him to lie upon it.

"I don't understand," he shook his head. "It looks like… a palace, or a room for a harem, or something."

"Well," her head bobbed around for a moment, "A palace, perhaps; a harem, not so much." She faced him squarely. "We have evolved beyond being physical creatures; pleasures of the flesh are less stimulating than those of the mind." With a graceful wave of her hand, she indicated one of the couches. Taking a seat, she patted the cushion next to her and softly said, "Join me, Charlie."

He sat at the opposite end, leaving a length of cushion between them. Curling her legs beneath her, she leaned comfortably into the corner and waited. Kicking off his shoes, he drew his legs up as well, ensuring she kept her distance.

"This is nice," he grinned, hoping that he appeared at ease.

"Open your mind to me, Charlie," she implored.

He inhaled deeply and blew the breath out through a relaxed jaw. "I'm ready," he replied softly.

"Good, because I have shown you much. What did you see, back at the playground?"

"I saw some kid get beat up by some other boys," he stated flatly.

"Yes, he got exactly what he deserved. A bully, bullied. That is my purpose, Charlie. You see, when Keeper and I first came to this world, we saw in it great promise. But to reach that promise, we believed that one side must never be allowed to overtake the other."

"You mean the darkness and the light," he supplied what he knew.

"Exactly," she agreed. "In the world that we came from, there is no darkness," she wafted her hand, indicating the room in which they sat. "There is only light, and joy, and comfort."

"What's wrong with that?" Charlie demanded, almost angrily. "Shouldn't people be allowed t' be happy? To not have some kid or person picking on them an' beating them up?"

"Oh, Charlie," she smiled, "You fail to see; there can be no light without the darkness. Happiness does not bring pleasure without the understanding of pain, of sadness, and despair."

He stared at her, rolling his tongue around as he considered the concept. "So your sayin' that we can't define one without the other."

"Yes," she nodded. "Our world had lost something, in the elimination of sorrow and suffering. We had become complacent; bored with our existence."

"So you came here, an' started mucking things up."

She burst into a loud laugh, "We have done no such thing. We have merely ensured that neither side will win. Keeper holds the balance, and our children champion their sides."

"Your children!" he sat straight up as he screamed, "You mean Destiny and Fate are *your* kids?"

"Of course," a glass of wine appeared in her hand, and she took a slow sip from the beverage. "But not in the physical sense that you understand of propagation. Keeper and I are ancient beings, and we created our children with the purpose each has been given."

She paused, getting to her feet and pacing in front of him, her clothing shifting to a long red robe that flowed around her. Watching her, Charlie's mind raced; *the devil is a woman in a red dress.*

"I am not the devil!" she snapped.

Shit. He hated being around people who could read his thoughts. "I'm sorry, it's just a saying, that's all." He felt surprisingly calm, having heard her story thus far, but after all the crazy things he had already experienced; *meh.* He wasn't impressed.

"So, you and Keeper came here, made your kids, and basically took over."

Sighing loudly, she shook her head. "Not exactly, but that version will do."

"Ok, then why have you brought me and the other Forgotten Angels here? Are we your servants, like the Summer Angels to Destiny and the Dark Angels to Fate?"

Staring at him, her voice quavered, "You are not an angel, Forgotten or otherwise. Where did you hear that name?" she demanded, stepping closer to tower over him.

"I made it up," he admitted, a little afraid for the first time since he had arrived there. "Look, I didn't mean anything by it," he tried to stand, but she blocked him, keeping him seated on the pliable surface. "I just thought it fit; we have powers, we've seen the other side, but we don't really belong, like someone forgot about us."

Her hands on her hips, she stepped back, making a slow circle in the large room. "Yes, I see," she whispered loudly, "You understand more than I had suspected." Looking up at him, she didn't mince words; "I need you, Charlie."

Thinking he had just been propositioned, he leapt to his feet. Holding his hands out in front of him, he growled, "Now wait a minute -"

"Not like that!" she laughed, cutting him off. Stepping towards him, she grasped his trembling digits firmly. "I mean that I need your talent; your understanding." Seeing his confusion, she continued, "I like that,

Forgotten Angels; and you are exactly right, the other plane has more or less forgotten about us. They don't care that we are here, and we are unimportant to them. We are not the darkness, nor are we the light; we are the combination of the two, where the lines meet and are blurred. But we will have our day, with you on our side; I guarantee it!"

EIGHT

Karma Knows Best

CHARLIE STARED at the woman before him as if she were sprouting extra limbs. "Why is everyone in your world so damned interested in me?" *This is the third time one of them has insinuated I should side with them!*

"It's your world, too," she soothed, rubbing the back of his hand with her fingertips. Turning it palm up, she swiped it a few times. "Charlie, listen to me. I know that you think we have hurt people, by being here, but that's really not our intention."

"I thought you were here to punish people," he quipped.

"I am," she stammered, "but that's only because that's the job I took. We wanted to care for this place; to see that it didn't end up like our home, with nothing to live for. Without challenges to face, life has no meaning, no reason to grow or develop." She cut her eyes up at him, then raised her chin to meet his gaze squarely.

"Ok," he shrugged, her deep brown orbs getting the better of him. "Is that why you keep your kind a secret?"

"Yes," she agreed, dropping his hand and turning away, "If we are discovered, it changes everything. It's happened a few times, and the consequences have been disastrous. We put a few rules into place when the twins took on their roles, but accidents happen."

Staring at her long auburn waves, Charlie considered his previous knowledge on the subject; *secrets were shared, and many paid the price.* "Did you punish the ones who did it?"

"I punished everyone, hun," she admitted quietly. "Have you ever heard of the black death?"

"You mean the plague?" his voice rose at the thought of it.

"Yes," she turned to him once more, "I unleashed it. It was the only way I could contain the spread of the leak. Mankind was not meant to know about our existence, and it must remain so at all cost."

"I get it," he agreed with a huff of air. "So if I agree to this, what would my job be?" he asked, still tempted to tell her to piss off, and take the prison route.

Shaking her head, she sighed, "Please don't make me hurt you. I know what's good for you, and I want you to have a good life. If you refuse, then I will be forced to motivate you..." her voice trailed away.

"Motivate me, as in with a stick or some other form of torture?" An instant after he said it, images of his mother appeared in his mind's eye. "No, you wouldn't!"

"Don't push me, Charlie," she gritted her teeth. "I can be fair, or I can play dirty; I'm good either way."

Staring at her with his mouth agape, he understood why Phil had been so upset with her. *I wonder what she did to him.*

"I didn't do anything to him," she answered the unasked question, her eyes growing a shade lighter. "You've talked with the others; you've seen how it is. We can do this the easy way, or we can do it the hard way, but we *are* going to do it. You will serve me, and do my bidding, or I won't have to look very far to find something or someone that matters to you."

Turning, her gown swirling around her, she glided across the room. Each of the four walls held a pair of curtains; fake windows he presumed. Pulling on a cord hanging down the side of one, the drapes parted, exposing a pane of glass; but instead of seeing the desert through the opening, he could see a short plump girl cleaning tables at what appeared to be a diner.

"Tabs," Charlie breathed, recognizing the best friend who had shared his life for so long. "Why are you showing me this; what does it mean?" he demanded curtly.

"It's time to get to the bottom line," she wafted her hand at the scene. "It's my job to see that people get what they deserve, and these monitors help me keep track of who has earned privileges... and who needs to be punished." She cut her eyes over at him and smiled deviously. "But, there is only so much of me and my minions to go around; sometimes it takes a while to catch up with everyone."

"So Tabs has done somethin', and you're gonna punish her," he deduced.

"Oh no," Karma grinned wickedly, "Tabitha hasn't done anything I'm interested in dishing out. However, her father has been skating along for a while..." her voice trailed away as she turned her attention back to the oversized screen.

"Uh-huh," Charlie knew it was true; his mind briefly wandered, recalling the drunken mess that was Tabitha Turner's dad. "So what're you gonna do to him?"

Cutting her eyes over at him, Karma's deep brown orbs swirled with a soft green taking its place in them. "You know the rules, Charlie. I can't attack him directly, but I can send a bit of justice his way."

"No, don't!" his voice thundered. "Her mom left, and her dad's all that she's got. It would devastate her t' lose him..." he surmised the worst was coming.

Her smile shifted into a warm grin, "My my, you do have so many targets. People you wouldn't want to see suffer. So unlike the young man I remember."

"You remember," he took a half step back, not really surprised that she, too, had watched him as a child. "Look, why don' you just tell me what you want."

"I want your allegiance," she stated calmly. "You have a great power, Charlie. Things are changing, and time is running out. Pledge yourself to my cause, and you will be rewarded. But, should you cross me, the consequences would be most severe," she flicked her eyes over at the girl, who now stood behind the register.

"If I do that, I want something else in return," his chest expanded and he clenched his fists tightly.

Noting his posture, she nodded slowly, "Name it."

"I want you out of my head; and Lorren. I want a shield that protects my thoughts and keeps them private."

"Ohhh," she turned her back, hiding her wide grin. "Aren't you the clever one. All right, so long as you are faithful to your oath, you will have protection against telepathy; no one will invade your mind. Not even Phil will be able to detect anything from you."

"And if I break my vow to serve you?" he asked cautiously.

"I'll know it the instant that it happens," she stood up straighter, facing him squarely. "Your thoughts will betray you."

Watching the customers leave the counter, Charlie observed his friend for long moment. "And you won't touch anyone that I care about, for as long as I'm with you."

"Right," Karma nodded. "That's a given."

"And I get Clarisse back," he pushed for more.

Blinking rapidly a few times, her jaw grew tight, but she had already promised him that and reluctantly agreed, "Yes; she will be returned to you when you have completed a satisfactory number of tasks."

"Then I guess that will have to do; if I have your word on that."

"You have my word," she flicked her hand and darkened the device on the wall, drawing the shade over it once more. "You will make your oath to me now. Kneel down."

Glancing around anxiously, Charlie placed his left knee on the floor, and balanced with his right leg folded to form a lap to rest his hands on. "Like this?"

"That will do," she stepped closer, her long fingers reaching his scalp and slithering through his hair.

He could feel a tingle that tickled his entire being. Waiting, he breathed deeply, feeling lighter, as if he could step outside his body and watch. "What are you doing?" he asked softly.

"Shh," she quieted him. "We are joined in a way no human can understand. Your soul, the essence of your being is pledged to me. I will guide you, and release all that you are capable of, for Karma is the ultimate teacher."

Laying his head back, his neck stretched, he felt drawn to the beauty of her strong features and noted the green of her eyes that almost glowed in the dimly-lit room. "I am yours," he breathed.

NINE

Lying with Dogs

THE SUN HAD SET when Charlie exited Karma's dwelling. The evening air cool, he made his way to the house, grateful that his thoughts were once again private. He had no words to describe what she had done to him, and he felt ashamed that he had enjoyed the mingling of their beings. *They don't have sex,* he mused; *they go way beyond it.* He had become joined with her in a way he never thought possible.

Letting himself inside, he crossed the dark rooms quietly and opened the massive refrigerator in search of food. Bathed in the glow of the small light, he jumped when the overhead bulbs burst to life.

"So, you've gotten to see the inside of Karma's love nest," Phil announced loudly, crossing the room and leaning over the counter that separated the kitchen from the dining area to rest his chin on his fists.

"What's it to you?" Charlie growled, in no mood to be taunted for the tough choices he had been forced to make.

Staring at him, Phil rolled his tongue for a moment, then bit sourly, "So was it good for you?"

"I don't kiss and tell," the younger man clipped, his heart beating faster at the memory of his first supernatural tryst.

Frowning, Phil stood up straighter. "How are you doing that?" he demanded loudly.

Ignoring him, Charlie selected his items and closed the fridge. Taking his food to the table, he opened the dishwasher with his mind and floated a plate and fork over to him, smiling when they had landed safely on the wooden surface beside him.

"Hey, I'm talking to you," Phil stepped towards him, slamming his hand down on the table and rattling the dishes upon it.

Opening the containers and serving his plate, Charlie remained unmoved. When his portions were ready, he floated the platter to the microwave, opening the door and even setting the timer remotely. "I'm really getting better at this," he grinned, feeling a bit happy to be able to use his powers openly.

"What's going on down here?" Lorren asked in a small voice, her fluffy house shoes scraping softly on the tile of the kitchen floor.

Phil crossed his arms over his muscular chest, "Charlie's been lying with dogs," he informed her crassly. "He musta really enjoyed it, cause he's got nothing to say about it."

Feeling the hot flush of anger working its way up his neck to his face, Charlie growled, "You should watch what you say, Phil. Karma an' I are gettin' t' be pretty good friends."

"Like you're the first, or the only one for that matter," Phil shot back. "Karma's like a door knob around here; we all get our turn."

"Eww," Lorren squealed, putting a glass on the counter and filling it with milk. "Men are disgusting; and you wouldn't get in near as much trouble if you learned to shut up once in a while," the girl informed him.

Bringing his plate to the table in the same manner he had placed it in the microwave, Charlie sat down and stabbed a few bites of the leftover roast. Taking the seat at the end, the girl studied him, her eyes clouded with confusion. "I can't reach you," she finally admitted softly.

"Yeah," Charlie agreed. "Karma made me a deal. As long as I'm a good boy, you guys can't read my thoughts or feelings or any of that shit," he spat. "I'm not too keen on people being in my head, if you get what I mean."

"Is that why you joined her? To protect yourself?" Phil stood up straighter, "Well, I got news for you. It's not going to, and even better news; if you thought taking Karma's side would get you out of trouble with Keeper, you're dead wrong." Stomping out of the room and up the stairs, he left the two young people to enjoy their midnight snack in peace.

Staring after him between bites, Charlie's mind raced. Finally, he said aloud, "I wonder what he meant by that. I thought Karma and Keeper were on th' same side; the one that keeps mankind in check, with the dark and light, an' all that stuff."

Shaking her head slowly, Lorren whispered, "Don't think too much about it, Charlie. It'll drive you crazy if you do. You picked Karma, and you can't go back on that now, so don't worry about Keeper."

"So they're not on the same side?" he replied gruffly.

"I don't really know," she shivered.

"So tell me about drowning," he scowled, recalling that Clarisse had drowned twice, more or less.

"I was five," she replied, running her fingers over her glass to collect the moisture forming there. "But, I was rescued, after I had been dead for about ten minutes. Everyone was so happy; my parents… everyone. But after that, I heard voices," she sniffled. "When my parents realized that they were hearing me inside their heads, they had me committed. Karma killed them, and rescued me from the hospital."

Frozen in mid-bite, Charlie stared at her. "She killed your parents?"

"She had to," the girl informed him softly. "It's against the rules for outsiders to know about us; any of us. I don't blame her for protecting her world; there's a lot at stake here, and you'll understand when you learn more about it."

Doubtful, Charlie ate for a few minutes, then continued, "So what is it that we do for Karma, exactly?" When she only stared at him, he pushed, "Come on; I'm going to find out soon enough anyways. She's going to start training me to be her minion."

Swallowing, the girl's eyes grew wide. "When Karma decides someone needs to be dealt with, good or bad, she gives the assignment to one of us. We go, and see that justice is served."

"Hmm," he took a swig of his tea to wash down the last of his meal. "The Forgotten Angels settle the score."

"Forgotten Angels?" she queried.

"That's us," he grinned, "Karma said she liked that name; I made it up after I met Phil last year."

"Charlie, you are pretty weird; I'm not sure that you realize that," she giggled.

"How so?" he leaned back in his chair and patted his full belly.

"You just have a different air about you, almost like you're happy with all of this and the way things are turning out," her words cut a deep frown into his features. "I don't mean to hurt your feelings, but you really do seem to be enjoying yourself."

"Well, since you can't read my thoughts, that's just your opinion," he floated his plate over to the sink with a nonchalant wave of his hand. "Besides, I've known a few people who deserved to be punished," Charlie's mind flashed Brett Nelson for a moment, and the justice he had dispensed upon him the summer before put a genuine smile on his face. "I kinda like the idea, to be honest."

"I think you and Dante are going to be really good friends," she replied, getting to her feet; "If he doesn't kill you."

"Who's Dante?" he shot back.

"Dante *was* Karma's favorite minion. They used to spend a lot of time together in her little pleasure palace, if you get what I mean. And, she always sends him on the big assignments." Rinsing her glass, she laid it beside his plate in the basin and scooted towards the stairs. "If you're really getting that thick with her, it could spell trouble."

"Naw, I was just giving Phil a hard time. Karma an' I aren't really a thing. I'm gonna get my girl back, and Dante can keep bein' her main squeeze," he chuckled. When the girl disappeared up the stairs without a reply, he sat tapping the table before him for a few minutes, lost in thought. Eventually, he cleared the rest of the leftovers and returned them to the fridge. "Silly girl," he mumbled aloud. *As if Karma could ever really be interested in me; and I'm sure as hell not gonna get caught up on her.*

PART II
Karma's Revenge

Prologue

"CHARLIE," Phil spat, announcing himself as he strutted into his room.

"Yeah," the younger man's gaze remained on the morning sun outside. Relaxed in one of the two chairs that faced the window, his feet propped on the ledge below it, he appeared unmoved by Phil's arrival.

"Karma's sending you out with me today." Phil's arms crossed his chest, his displeasure at spending time with the new trainee obvious.

"Mmk," Charlie got to his feet. "I guess I'm providing the transportation?" he smirked.

Phil grunted, "Sure." He had been angry to discover that Karma taught Charlie more than she had the others, providing him with more than the single talent each member in the rest of the group possessed. Having him act as his transporter only rubbed salt in the wound.

"Fine; where are we headed?" Charlie changed his shirt casually.

"Syracuse, New York. I have a few rewards to bestow."

Charlie half grinned, aware that Phil preferred the cushier assignments. "Ok," he nodded, transporting them to a crowded mall. Spreading his hands, he teased, "How's this?"

"Funny," Phil shot back, telepathically amending his directions, again disgruntled that he could send signals to Charlie, but could not read anything from him unless the boy allowed it. Karma was playing favorites in Purgatory, and it did nothing to improve his attitude about being forced to serve her. "You know you're not supposed to drop us in populated locations. Someone might notice."

"Relax," Charlie teased. "Humans ignore what they don't understand; they don't see our magic." Picking up on their true destination, he reluctantly made the adjustment and landed them in the hallway of an office building. Looking in through the door of one of the compartments, a heavy man sat behind the desk, the piles of paper attesting to his disorganization. "I'll wait," he whispered to his companion.

Knocking on the frame, Phil made his way inside the cubical and introduced himself. Charlie turned his back, not really interested in what the other man could be up to. *Some shmuck rescued a kitten, or something,* he mentally joked. He had been out with Phil a few times and had discovered that the man never handed down punishments; only rewards for good deeds.

Inside, he could hear the pair of them talking about some guy named Gary, and gathered that Phil wanted the fat man to give him something. *Figures,* he scoffed, wandering down the hall. *The man's an empath and could do anything he wanted with that talent; what a waste of resources.* Charlie had found it cool a few weeks ago, when he first realized he could transport people and objects, the same as Kari; but having to hang out with Phil had put a definite damper on the experience.

Phones rang periodically in the offices that flanked him, and he peered into the rooms one by one. He had slowly come to realize he was no longer part of their world, and felt more like an outsider than he ever had before. Passing a few of the workers, he smiled and nodded, pretending he knew where he was going. If anyone questioned his being there, none of them mentioned it.

I'm ready to leave, Phil's voice interrupted his thoughts. Turning around, he could see his partner at the other end of the narrow passage, outside the office. Picking up on their next stop. Charlie sighed as he transported the both of them to a park on the other side of town. Choosing to heed the other man's advice, he placed them discreetly amongst a group of trees.

Moving to the edge of the foliage, they observed a couple with a young boy. The girl laughing loudly, she gathered the boy in her arms and swung him around, then tumbled to the ground.

"That's my target," Phil indicated the man with them.

Charlie observed that his partner wore a smile, perhaps the first genuine one he had ever seen on him. "What's he being rewarded for?"

"He's a fireman; saved lots of lives over the years. This last Christmas, he saved that little boy, and then he took them and her mother into his home," Phil beamed.

"Ohhh," Charlie moaned knowingly.

"Not like that," Phil cut him off. "Gerald Ford is an upstanding kind of man. Only, Candy there won't go any further because his job is dangerous. They both deserve to be happy."

"So, how are you going to fix that?" Charlie shook his head in disbelief. "You can't *make* her change her mind."

"Oh, I think she will. I arranged for Gary to get a promotion," he indicated the call his target had just answered. Looking as if he might explode, Phillip Parson didn't enjoy being part of Karma's minions very often, and therefore he savored the moments when he did. "Nice," he leaned against the tree next to him and sighed. "That's his boss. This very second, he's informing him that he'll be given a desk job as an investigator. It's what he's been hoping for, and she can't refuse to date him any longer."

The man before them ended the call, taking a knee next to his sweetheart. A moment later, she flung herself into his arms, knocking him over and squealing loudly. "Looks like she's pleased," Charlie conceded.

"Yeah; it's times like this that make all the crap Karma gives us worthwhile."

Shooting his superior a smirk, Charlie boasted, "It's still more fun to punish them."

"Says you," Phil righted himself, implying their upcoming destination. "Either way, we can get on with the next deserving soul."

TEN

A Little Payback

"Just relax," Karma's voice soothed, her soft laugh hanging in the air; "That's it, hun."

Inhaling deeply, Charlie dropped his head back and blew noisily at the ceiling above him. The exterior door into the kitchen opened unexpectedly, and he jerked his gaze towards it; "Hey, Lorren."

The girl did not reply, and instead marched across the room to the counter that held the coffee pot. Spinning around with her filled cup, she headed to the basement, passing through his body without hesitation.

"Holy shit!" he gasped.

"We're in the other plane," Karma grinned at him. "You have passed your final test."

Staring at his hands, as if they should be invisible, he stated cautiously, "I can't believe this's real."

"Believe it, baby," she chortled.

"Naw, you don't understand. Clarisse said that th' planes were divided; no one goes between them. I mean, I did what you said, an' obviously it worked," he looked up at her squarely, "I jus' don' understand why."

"Because you're special, Charlie," she flashed him her best smile. "The planes *are* divided, as they have been since Keeper and I first arrived here. There are only a handful of people who are not bound by that magic. Those who are strong enough to bend the rules."

Charlie had learned a great deal in his months at Purgatory. He had risen in the hierarchy, and only one other Forgotten Angel ranked above him. *No wonder Phil's jealous of me,* he mused, recalling their most recent venture to hand out rewards to do-gooders. He could see the pride in her eyes and had no doubt he would one day soon be her number one minion.

Turning his back on her and bouncing down the stairs, he made his way to the cubicles below. A large open area occupied the majority of the basement; a grid of sixteen small spaces that held a desk, chair, and computer in each of them, all divided by a honeycomb of short walls. At the far end stood Karma's lavish office, and his stall just before it.

Arriving at his space, he opened a drawer and pulled out his journal, where he had been keeping notes about his discoveries. Flipping through the pages to the first blank one, he noted the date, and then wrote in large block letters: *CROSSED THE PLANE.*

Clenching his jaw, he focused on the division, and could almost see it, as if it were a thin veil that hung over him for a moment, before it was snatched off of him with a whiff. Coughing, he noted the few other heads that occupied the room, watching them over the top of their chest-high dividers to gauge their reactions. When no one moved, he called loudly, "Hey, Lorren!" to the girl who occupied the stall directly across from him.

"Hey yourself," she retorted, not bothering to look up from her screen. She only had two hours of internet time per week, and she wasn't about to waste any of it messing with him.

Karma had casually followed him down and opened her office, her hips swaying as she moved. Leaving the door ajar, she waited for him to join her. "I think you're ready for a few assignments," she informed him when he did.

"Ok," his Adam's apple bobbed as he swallowed, "I guess you mean on my own?" He'd been partnering with others in the group of Forgotten Angels for the three months that he had been in Purgatory, but had never gone alone.

"Yeah," she smiled, nodding slightly. Dropping a manila folder on her desk, she opened it. "This is my special case file. Close the door, baby."

Obediently swinging the portal shut, he then moved around to stand beside her. Telepathically opening the set of red velvet curtains that covered her viewing screen, she began, "I have someone who needs a little payback." Indicating the young man, they observed as he strolled along the street, his hands in his pockets as he bopped along to some unheard music.

"What's he done?" Charlie folded an arm across his chest and put the other hand under his chin.

"He's a dealer," she shrugged, "One of many, I guess you know. But, he's taken up with a girl, and been giving some of his product to her kid."

"What a dick," his hands dropped, flying to his hips. "What do you want done with him?"

"I don't know," she grinned slyly, "You know I like it rough... go pay him a visit and see what you come up with."

"Yeah," Charlie snorted, anger boiling in his gut... *we like it rough.*

ELEVEN

Calling Home

THREE DAYS LATER, Charlie leaned back in his chair, the phone pressed against his ear firmly, "Everything's fine, mom." He couldn't see over the tops of the walls from that position, but he knew most of the cubicles were empty, save Lorren directly across the aisle. Pushing his fingers roughly through his hair, he waited.

"You don' sound like yourself," the woman on the other end insisted.

"I know, I'm just..." he hesitated, glancing through the narrow openings to see that his neighbor had stopped moving to listen. "I have to go."

"What do you mean you have t' go?" his mother screamed over the line.

"Mom, I told you. I'm not allowed t' talk about this place. All I can tell you is, I'm fine. I'm better than fine, actually," he grinned to himself. "I'm doin' meaningful work, an' I'm really glad that I came here."

"So you're workin' on those hours so you can come home soon?" Bethany sniffed.

"Yeah, I'll be home soon," he replied more softly. Tapping his pencil on the desk for a moment, he regretted the phone calls more with each week that passed. "Seriously, I have to go," he insisted.

"All right, baby," Beth agreed. "I'll talk to you again next week." Her voice filled with sadness, he could clearly tell that she missed him. "I love you, son," she whispered before she hung up.

Placing the handset in the cradle, Charlie released the breath he'd been holding loudly. Lorren stood to join him in his private space. "I don't call anyone," she informed him. "With my parents both gone, there's really no need. I didn't realize how lucky I was for that."

"Yeah," he agreed, bouncing the eraser end against the flat surface a few more times. "When I first came here, gettin' t' make the calls was my lifeline. Now," he paused, forming the words carefully. "Now, I wish I didn't have t' talk to her. It hurts her too much."

A commotion erupted at the far end of the giant room, at the base of the stairs, signaling that the rest of the Forgotten Angels had joined them. Glancing around quickly, Lorren anxiously darted over to her seat and dropped out of their line of sight.

Blinking a few times, Charlie's mind wandered, drifting over his sentencing and the first time that he had seen Karma. *Man, if I only knew the trouble I was getting into.* He wasn't allowed to tell his mother about Purgatory, or anything else about their world, and that was fine. *I wouldn't tell her anyways, even if I could,* he admitted to himself; she was better off not knowing the sinister details of his current existence.

His thoughts shifted to the dealer he had paid a visit to a few days before, grinning at the recollection of appearing next to him as he strutted down the street. *Such arrogance,* he had observed. Turning the corner, the man and his invisible companion had arrived at a set of steps leading up to a pair of entrances; a duplex. Skipping up the short incline, the young man had knocked sharply before opening the door and darting inside.

The front room of the structure barren, a few chairs and a folding table occupied the space. "You're late," the black man standing at the front windows growled.

"Sorry, Calvin," his target replied, "I was followed, so I took the long way."

"You got rid of 'em?"

"Yeah, I ditched 'em clean," he threw a leg over the top of one of the chairs, clearing it and dropping into the seat. "I need extra this week," he stated casually.

"Raul," his supplier turned slowly, "you got anything you wanna tell me?"

Watching the dark eyes staring up at him, Charlie observed the sweat forming on his brow. *Raul*, he noted to himself, moving about the room and inspecting the shabby surroundings. The silence grew more tense with each second that the seated man considered his response.

"Naw, man. We're cool. I just picked up some new business… you know," he finally offered.

"Yeah, I know," the man in charge pursed his lips and Charlie grinned, realizing it would be easy to set him against his target.

He had gotten used to the new rules, those that governed the Forgotten Angels. Karma had taught him well, and although he still needed practice with his growing talents, he enjoyed the feeling that using them supplied. He had been on a few missions to reward those who deserved it, but found the deepest pleasure came from punishing those driven by the darkness.

Another knock sounded at the door before it opened, and two men entered, pushing a young woman in ahead of them. *The plot thickens.* Charlie leaned against a wall, his pulse quick with anticipation.

"This is Ellen," Calvin indicated the girl. "But I guess you already knew that."

Raul ran his hands over his jeans to remove the sweat from his palms. His mahogany orbs darting from face to face, he waited, not bothering to reply.

Grinning, Charlie's brown eyes began to glow, a soft green filling them as he searched the dealer's thoughts. In an instant, he found the memory he wanted; one of Raul holding Ellen against a wall and driving his naked body against hers. Watching the recollection unfold, he could see the man in the chair squirm. *Yeah, he knows her*, Charlie chuckled. Jealousy would almost be cheating; *it's so easy to manipulate.*

Waving his hand slightly to improve his focus, he imparted the memory to the man in charge, allowing him to envision the particulars as Raul clutched a hand full of her hair; pulling it as he slammed against her. The sound of her loud moans practically filled the room as Calvin's teeth clenched, his muscled jaw flexing.

"You been bangin' my bitch?" he demanded, his fists pressed knuckles to knuckles in front of him.

"No, man," Raul stammered, "I'd never…"

Charlie laughed aloud, enjoying the smell of fear that tickled his nostrils. "Get him, Calvin," he whispered. In a flash, the large black form leapt across the narrow gap between them, knocking the seated man to the floor and pounding him with a heavy fist.

"Hey!" a hand shoved Charlie more firmly, shocking him back to Purgatory and the present.

"What?" he sneered up at the tan blond who towered over him.

"Karma's got a gig for us," Dante informed him curtly.

Getting to his feet, Charlie dropped the pencil he'd been chewing next to the phone, his mind briefly flashing his mother, who had been on the other end. *Thank God she doesn't know what I've been up to*, he thought wryly. A duality had settled over him in the three months that he had been there, living a life he would have been ashamed to reveal to her.

Part of him had been sad to lose his previous life; the one he had shared with Bethany Phillips. But most of him had come to enjoy the power he had over men; *that asshole got exactly what he deserved*, he praised himself as he stepped the few paces into Karma's office. He enjoyed being a wielder of justice and a bringer of pain.

I like this life, he sighed, closing the wooden portal behind him. Of course that meant calling home became less and less important as the days went by, and he felt certain at some point he would stop doing it all together.

TWELVE

Dante's Nemesis

DANTE WATCHED the other male close the door and join them. Using his fingers to fluff up his blond spikes, he squared his shoulders and faced the red-head behind the desk. She had been his boss for over a decade, and they had been looking for something, or someone, for the majority of the time. Still, when he had come home to Purgatory three months prior to find Charlie there, he had been a little stunned.

Karma looked up at the bronzed God before her, his muscles bulging against the seam of his shirt sleeve. At five-foot-five, she wasn't exactly short, but in her flats, his six-foot-four frame towered over her. "Thank you, darling," she cooed.

Squinting at her, he shot a glance over at Charlie before he spoke, "So, he's going with me on a special run?"

"Yes," her crimson-stained lips glistened, "Charlie has passed all of the prerequisites and completed his first priority mission."

"I see," he ran his hand across his hard chest, anxious before he extended the appendage and offered it politely. "I gotta hand it to you; I didn't really think you had it in you."

Shaking firmly, Charlie smiled, "Oh, I'm versatile."

Watching the exchange, Karma could have cut the tension in the room with a knife. She had promised Charlie not to invade his thoughts, and had so far refrained from doing so. At this point, she didn't need her powers to see that the two young men despised one another. "I hope this isn't going to be a problem," she stated firmly.

"Oh, hell no," Dante's lips curled, still eyeing his nemesis. He hadn't figured out how he was going to get rid of him, but he knew Charlie's days were numbered. "Give us the deets," he insisted.

"All right," she smoothed her bright red skirt over her behind and sat calmly, "Have a seat, gentleman." Indicating the view screen over their shoulders, the curtain that hid it most of the time shifted, and they turned so they could watch.

Charlie listened to the briefing for the most part, his pulse strong in his neck. Cutting his eyes over, he could see that his counterpart covertly watched him as well. *I wonder how strong he is*, he pondered. If he ever hoped to make it to the head of the group and be Karma's right hand man, Dante would have to be dealt with.

He had been out with all of the Forgotten Angels on missions over the last few months; *all but him*. Karma had kept them separated, like two male tigers she didn't want fighting over her. *I guess she thinks I'm ready for the challenge.*

Forcing his mind back to the task at hand, he caught the words *this needs to be brutal*. Twisting to face her, he inquired, "How brutal?"

"I want them to suffer," she sneered. "These guys have been happy to do Fate's bidding, and they're regular pawns of a few Dark Angels. It's time to make them pay."

Charlie's mind turned, recalling the lengthy discussion he had held with himself when he first realized that Karma seemed to be targeting those who were clients or minions of the Light and Dark Angels. Her purpose still eluded him, and he occasionally felt a smidge of guilt at their actions; *they're just doin' what they're told or made to do*, he rationalized. *Why punish them for that?*

Meeting his gaze, Karma waited for him to signal his agreement to the task.

"We got this, miss," Dante stood, eager to demonstrate his loyalty. "Don't worry about your new pet... I won't let anything happen to him."

Charlie rose stiffly, "I'm not her pet."

"Boys," she called sharply, "I won't tolerate fighting among the ranks." She clasped her hands together in front of her face, darkening the screen and closing the velvet cover. "And don't think that I am going to punish one of you and not the other," her eyes darted between them. "If you can't work this out, you will both suffer my wrath."

The door swung open, and she indicated it by extending her long fingers towards it. "Be on your way, and let me know when you're in position to begin the assault."

"Yes ma'am," Dante nodded at her. "Let's go, boy," he called over his shoulder as he marched out of the room.

Charlie didn't follow. Instead, he transported himself to his dorm, two flights above them. Leaning on the bunk above his bed, he sighed loudly; *Jesus Christ*. He had gotten used to the slight dizziness the action produced, but sometimes it still got the better of him, especially when he was flustered.

He had doubted Karma's word when she first began training him; that he was special. He had been moving objects with his mind for over a year, but had no idea how deeply the gift ran within him. When she taught him how to teleport, it had been as if a flood gate had been opened, pouring the magic and abilities out of him in a raging torrent.

Realizing he wasn't alone, he glanced up to find Kari seated in one of the chairs. "Hey," he addressed his roommate with a small wave.

"You ok, mate?" his friend nodded in return.

"Yeah," Charlie stammered, pretending to straighten the bunk he had used to support him. "Dante an' I are goin' on a run together; a big one. Not sure how long we'll be gone," he offered casually.

"Watch yourself," Kari warned. "Dante's... well, Dante. He doesn't like you, mate."

"I know," Charlie grimaced in return. "I don't think he likes anyone."

"Well, if you weren't after his spot, it might be different," Kari laughed, then vanished, leaving him to prepare for his journey in peace. Charlie stared at the vacated seat, wondering if everyone knew about their point of contention.

Down stairs, Dante had felt the shimmer as soon as Charlie disappeared. Spinning on his heel, he reclosed the door behind him to keep their confrontation private. "Karma, whatever I did, I'm sorry," he began.

Smiling up at him, she opened herself to him, allowing him to connect with her mind, "Have you missed me, baby?"

"Desperately," he breathed, catching her hand and kissing her palm over the top of the desk that stood between them. "God, it's been so long."

"I know, love," she grasped his digits firmly, transporting them both to her haven.

Finding himself standing inside what essentially was her boudoir, with her smaller body next to him, he pulled her against him. "Oh, Karma," he whispered into her hair. He knew she had been entertaining herself with Charlie ever since the younger man's arrival, but he didn't care; he wanted her as if he were an addict and she were his drug.

"Shh," she soothed, running her hands up his body and guiding him to kneel before her.

His breath quickened with anticipation. What Karma could do to a man no human female could match. Where any old girl could set a man's skin on fire, she could set his mind and soul ablaze. Her fingers against his scalp, he whimpered, "Please don't stop."

Taking in slow, deep pants, Karma mingled their spirits, separating him from his physical form. "Do you serve me?" she hissed.

"I serve you," his voice echoed her desperation.

Her grip tightened, then relaxed against his follicles, stimulating his mind as the energy of their beings expanded into the air around them. The room grew bright with millions of tiny pinpoints of light, the particles of their souls being swirled above them as they were mixed. A moment later, an explosion sent them flying away from the center of the empty room.

THIRTEEN

Red-Headed Stepchild

"THIS IS IT," Dante indicated the buildings below them with an open palm.

Standing on an incline next to him, Charlie surveyed the structures. The largest, and clearly a house, appeared run down and badly in need of paint. The barn closest to them also had lost most of its protective coating, exposing grey wood beneath the remaining red. "I don't see anyone," he commented, taking a few steps down the slope.

"Well, they're around here somewhere," Dante followed, using his muscular legs to push his way through the thick brush. Checking out the stand of trees that flanked the compound, they snaked along the path in silence.

Arriving at the flat ground where a smaller shed stood away from the other two buildings, they paused. Inside, they picked up on a few muffled sounds. "Yeah, I hear 'im," Charlie agreed.

Passing through the wall, the pair peeked inside to find a man in a dirty white tee-shirt and jeans rummaging through a selection of tools. Appearing to find what he wanted, he stood up straight and swung around, facing them squarely. Marching through the pair of them, he exited, slamming the wooden covering behind him.

Following the bald head, Charlie commented quietly, "This whole plane business is still a bit hard t' fathom." He recalled that he had seen people on the other side when he was boy. "Have you ever felt like one of them could see you, or knew you were there?"

"Naw, man," Dante shot him a quick glance. "It'd be like winning the lottery, finding one of them who could see into this side, as you put it."

"As I put it," Charlie pulled up short as their target entered the barn, then trailed him into the dim interior. "How would you describe it?"

"We're in the same place that they are. And, we're experiencing the same world, but," Dante paused, looking around the room at the stacks of assorted supplies. Moving over to inspect what turned out to be large bags of fertilizer, he grimaced. "It's more like we have a protective barrier that keeps them from noticing us, and allows them to pass through us."

"Like a cloaking device," Charlie mocked him while running his fingers through the dark, loose material from one of the bags. "You think they have a garden around here?"

"Not that I saw. This isn't here to make plants grow," Dante turned, watching the man combine a few of the items into a mixture over at a long wooden table. "I think he's making bombs."

"Bombs?" Charlies voice rose an octave momentarily before he reeled it back down. "Are you sayin' these guys are terrorists?"

Cutting his eyes over at him, Dante snorted, "Weren't you listening to what Karma said in the briefing?"

Glancing around guiltily, Charlie shoved his hands in his pockets, "I may have drifted off."

"Really," the other man scoffed, turning his back on him and wandering around the shack. "Don't make a habit of that." A moment later, he paused, demanding loudly, "She couldn't tell you weren't listening?"

"What do you mean?" the younger man's eyes grew wide in surprise.

"I mean, when you weren't paying attention, she couldn't tell you were thinking about something else?" A pair of men joined them at that moment, carrying a few canisters of some liquid and placing them on the floor next to the table.

Feeling vulnerable, Charlie left the barn, under the pretense of looking around outside. Hot on his heels, Dante demanded loudly, "Answer me, dammit! I thought you had connected with her." Maybe his understanding of things had been all wrong from the start.

"I did, I guess," Charlie stopped to face him squarely, "But afterwards, I asked her to stay outta my head. And t' keep anyone else from invadin' my thoughts; my *personal* space," he bit the word personal angrily. "Or haven't you noticed?" he accused.

Dante couldn't believe his ears. "I wouldn't know about your head; I have no reason to share with you, or listen for that matter," the taller man lied flatly. He had tried to access Charlie early on, but had taken his well-protected consciousness as an indicator of his ability. "So you don't share with her telepathically?"

"No, I don't," he replied while watching a truck and car moving slowly up the long driveway.

"Huh," Dante shrugged, aware that the ramifications of this discovery could be huge. "I like being connected to her," he informed his companion crisply, not sure what her protecting the new-comer really indicated.

"Well, I don't," Charlie pointed at the approaching vehicles. "This don' look good. What do you suppose they're up to, exactly?" Three men piled out of the truck, and another pair exited the car, dragging a young woman along with them. Taking a single step closer, a cold chill rippled through him, despite the afternoon sun beating down on his brown waves.

Noting the girl's hands were bound and her eyes covered, he watched two of the men flank her and haul her up the few steps into the farm house. Swallowing, he wondered if Karma had said anything else he had missed that would explain why they were holding the girl.

"We need to check in," Dante spat, leaping onto the veranda and peering into the front through the dirty windows. Smiling broadly, his voice grew lighter, "Oh, there you are." Realizing Charlie couldn't hear her, he tapped the glass before them, and an image of Karma in her pristine red suit became visible.

"Thanks, babe," she smiled at him over the connection.

"You didn't tell me your new toy was squeamish," Dante laughed loudly.

"I'm not squeamish," Charlie bit back, moving so he could see their leader more clearly. "That's a neat trick; does it work on any glass?"

"Pretty much," Karma agreed. "I'll have to teach you that one when you get back to Purgatory. For now, are you ready to take care of these guys?"

"It's not just our targets," Dante informed her bluntly. "A few of them showed up a few minutes ago with a girl; bound and blind folded."

"Cut her loose before you act," Karma grimaced, closing her eyes for a moment. When they reopened, a glimmer of pain flickered across them for an instant.

"What's wrong?" Charlie demanded, genuinely concerned.

"Nothing," the woman shot back quickly. "Charlie, you go inside and set her free as soon as they leave her alone. Make sure none of them see you do it. Then you two can finish the plan and get out of there."

"What if they don't leave her alone?" Dante demanded.

"They will," Karma exhaled loudly. "You may have to wait a few days before you get your chance; until then, find out everything you can to set up for the show."

"The show," Charlie repeated quietly, a sick feeling in his gut.

"Yes ma'am," Dante agreed, tapping the glass to remove the image. "You go on in and see what's going on with the girl. I'm going to have a better look around the barn and the shed; figure out exactly what we're going to do with these guys." Strutting across the planks as if he fully expected the younger man to carry out his orders, he trotted down the steps and through the weed-filled yard once more.

Swallowing hard, Charlie watched until Dante disappeared into the barn as he thought about what he might find on the other side of the wall. Cautiously moving to the door, he drew a deep breath, then passed through the frame. His sneakers squeaked on the hard wood of the floor, his heart pounding in his ears.

Inside, a large living area stretched out before him. The furniture sparse and ratty in appearance, he couldn't imagine anyone actually sitting on any of it. Straight through the front room, he could see a door he surmised led to the kitchen and dining area. Becoming aware of the rhythmical groan that a bed makes when a couple is on it, he turned his attention to the stairs that descended from above, forming a landing to his left.

His eyes tracing the steps slowly, he could make out the grunts of a man, and the girl squealed loudly. The sound of a slap on bare skin caused him to jump when a sharp scream followed before it became muffled. *Holy shit.* His gaze on the top of the stairs, he knew the young woman was up there somewhere, and he felt helpless.

Karma said to wait until she's alone, he reminded himself while clenching his fists. But the idea of what the men were doing to her tore at him, and he felt nauseous. Leaving the entrance, he stomped towards the kitchen, only to discover the noises from directly below the bedroom had not improved.

Hearing the distinct sound of a headboard smacking against a wall, he pressed his palms over his ears and hummed to block it out. Spying another exit, leading out to the field of weeds and wildflowers beyond, he darted through it and skipped down the steps; determined to wait at a distance.

"What are you doing out here?" Dante demanded when he discovered the boy sitting, leaned against a tree a short time later. "You're supposed to be inside, waiting to get her out of there!"

"I can't," Charlie stammered, his face drawn. "I'll go back in when they come out, but I can't stay in there and listen to them…. abuse her."

Only then picking up on his meaning, the leader of their duo paused, his mouth open for a moment before he snapped it shut. "Disgusting bastards," he fumed.

"Yeah, they're a real bunch o' savages. Wha's the plan for dealing with them?" Charlie changed the subject.

Dropping onto the ground next to him, Dante indicated the barn. "The guys out there are definitely building explosives. I'm thinking I can set them off and blow this whole place up around them." Glancing over at his comrade, he could see the paleness of his flesh. "You ok?"

"No," Charlie shook his head, his eyes still fixed on the window and the men moving around inside. "The last time I felt like this," he hesitated, shaking his head slightly, "I killed someone," he concluded.

Nodding, Dante didn't push, and merely agreed, "Well, they deserve it."

"Who are they, exactly?" Charlie pulled his knees up and wrapped his arms around them, resting his chin on the top, still eyeing their targets.

"They're some kind of hate group is all I can guess," Dante's voice grew softer, taking on a comforting tone. "Karma said they've been helping the Dark Angels. I'm sure that's the reason she sent us."

"To punish them," Charlie deduced. "Karma loves her revenge."

"Yeah, I guess," Dante shrugged. "But I'm sure it's more focused on Fate and his minions than these guys."

"What do you mean?" the younger man tilted his head so that he stared at him instead.

"I mean, she punishes humans from time to time, but her real focus is on her own kind; squaring things with them." He shifted uncomfortably after he spoke, then tacked on, "You know, Karma's family has treated her pretty badly. They deserve it as well."

Charlie's brow furrowed as he considered his cohort's words. "She said that she and Keeper made the twins; like their children."

"Yeah, she told me the same thing," Dante agreed, getting to his feet.

"So, what else did she tell you?" Charlie insisted, also standing.

"Not really anything. Mostly, she taught me how to use my gifts, same as you," the taller man glanced away, taking in the top of the ridge that ran behind them. "I think we should have a peek from the top before the sun sets; see what else is around here."

Following him into the line of trees, the pair came out of the grove and into a clearing at the crest. Peering around, they could see no evidence of people anywhere near them, save the winding dirt road that led back to the gathering of buildings they were waiting to destroy.

Watching the sun sink low from that vantage point, Dante picked up their earlier dialogue; "You should be careful."

"I should? Why?" Charlie shifted his weight anxiously.

"Karma's been looking for you for a long time," his comrade

informed him quietly. "I had really begun to doubt that you really existed, but obviously you do." Turning to face him, he blinked a few times. "I don't really like sharing her," he said more forcefully.

"Hey, look man," Charlie held up his hands in self-defense, "I'm not here for Karma. I really don't care about her, ok? Not like that."

"What do you care about?" Dante challenged, taking a seat in the dirt and watching the men moving around below them.

Staring at the horizon, Charlie could feel his chest grow tight. "I had a girl," he confessed quietly. "A Summer Angel. She's the love of my life." He looked down to see that his companion stared up at him, and their eyes locked on one another. "I want her back."

"So that's how she owns you," Dante broke the connection. "She owns all of us. Promises and punishments; that's how she keeps everyone in line."

"I've gathered that," Charlie took a seat on a large rock a few feet away. "The Forgotten Angels follow her, but not all of them are happy about it." He thought of Phil, and his hatred of their benefactor, even though he obviously enjoyed rewarding the worthy. *No wonder he tried to warn me to stay away from her.*

"Forgotten Angels," Dante snorted, "That name's pretty slick, by the way. Karma said you thought of it," he grinned at his companion. "Appropriate in so many ways."

"How so?"

"Karma's the red-headed stepchild in their world; no one really thinks about her, or cares about her. She helped to set everything up for Keeper and the twins, but..." he paused, giving a small nod, "They left her alone for too long."

"But Keeper's her husband, or mate, or something like that."

"No, not really. They were partners, and as soon as he had what he wanted, Keeper discarded her. Dropped her like a bad habit, and she's pretty bent out of shape about it."

A glimmer of understanding ignited in the back of Charlie's mind. Seeing the men all entering the house, he grunted. "Guess we're down for the night. I could go for a meal."

"Yeah, let's pop back to civilization and grab some dinner. These guys aren't going anywhere; at least not at the moment, and we can pick up here again in the morning," Dante suggested.

Following without argument, the pair vanished from the top of the hill and traveled to an all-night truck stop to eat and wait for the chance to execute their plan.

FOURTEEN

Karma's Good Side

TRANSPORTING INSTANTLY TO A DINER, the pair waited outside for a few minutes, checking out their surroundings. A large parking lot lay behind the structure, filled with trucks, most with their windows darkened. The visible light around a few edges indicated they were occupied with drivers who were down for the night.

"I think we're good," Dante informed him, crossing the plane so they could go inside.

Following his lead, Charlie made the move as well and they entered through the pair of glass doors in the front. Taking a booth along the exterior wall, he sighed loudly as he slid onto the cushioned seat. Through the glass, he could see the total black of the dark sky in the distance, and imagined the stars that were obscured by the lights of the town.

"I'm curious where they came from," he admitted softly after giving the waitress their order, observing a blue and green bruise on her jawline that she had tried to hide with her makeup.

"I used to be," Dante agreed, raising one shoulder with a shrug. Turning a palm to the ceiling, he sneered, "Would it do you any good if you knew?"

"I don' know," Charlie's eyes remained fixed on the girl.

Twisting in his seat, Dante followed his line of sight. "Yeah, he beats her."

Startled, Charlie hissed, "You know what I'm thinking?"

"I can't read you, if that's what you mean; but I can read her. And I've noticed you have a soft spot for girls in trouble," he grinned at his companion slyly. "Any reason why?"

Turning back to the darkness, Charlie thought about his life; the one he had lived before he discovered the existence of angels. Eating their food when it arrived in silence, he formulated his reply.

When his burgers and fries were gone, he spoke softly, telling his companion about Tabs. "My best friend growing up was a girl named Tabitha. Her old man was a real piece o' crap; drunken wife-beater. I don' think he took much out on her, but it messed her an' her life up. She's the one Karma threatened to hurt if I didn' cooperate when she brought me t' Purgatory."

Dante leaned his head back, looking down his nose at the man across from him. "So you take a woman getting knocked around, or whatever, a bit personally."

"Yeah," Charlie nodded, his eyes back on the girl whose behavior had shifted to anxious. She dropped a fork and balanced her load of dirty dishes to kneel down and retrieve it. Delving into her mind, he could feel the terror. Blocking it out, he searched, locating the source of her pain. "You mind if we make a quick detour?"

"You thinking about a side job?"

"Wouldn't take long," Charlie tapped the table nervously. "Would Karma care if we moved against an unassigned target?"

"Naw," Dante pursed his lips, shaking his head slightly. Charlie had only been with the group a few months. The fact that he took his role seriously and had sought out a deserving individual would actually win him brownie points with their leader. "As long as you only give out what they have coming, she'd be pleased," he admitted deviously. He had wanted to get rid of his nemesis, and wasn't about to miss the opportunity to do so.

Charlie's smile spread slow across his face. "I'm not really into pleasing her," he chuckled, "But I think that girl's boyfriend could use a little payback."

Having located her address and then his whereabouts, Charlie abandoned his search of her personal space and stood. Dropping a tip on the table, he demanded tartly, "You coming?"

"Sure," Dante grinned broadly, eager to see what the rookie would do. "I'm not going to help, but I can't wait to see you handle this guy."

Outside, Charlie transported them across town to a local dive as soon as they had crossed the plane and were no longer visible to ordinary humans. Arriving in a smoke-filled room, music thumped loudly around them. "This is where he'll be," he informed his cohort. "While she works, he's here hangin' out with his friends."

Locating the man easily, Charlie watched him for a few minutes. Seeing that this might take a while, Dante found a stool. He had sensed Karma watching them, and knew the younger man had trod onto dangerous ground. Where he could earn respect by taking his job to heart, he could also get himself into trouble. The key would always be to stay on Karma's good side, and he briefly considered that his opportunity to get rid of him could be at hand.

Moving through the rowdy patrons, Charlie studied his target and the men around him. Playing a game of pool, they were laying a folded bill on the table at the start of each game, wagering on the outcome. His eyes shifted from dark brown to the color of honey, taking on a green hue.

Two of the men at the table next to him immediately took an interest in his target's game. "That's it," Charlie mumbled, his lips curling when one of the observers finally took a swing with his wooden cue. The fight escalated quickly, engulfing a few others, who used chairs and glass bottles to inflict their disgruntled blows.

His eyes bright, Charlie could feel the elation in his chest. Watching the waitress' boyfriend take a beating, he thought about the morning he had used a napkin holder to crush a man's skull; an act he still felt guilt over. *But in the end, we all get what we deserve.*

Locating Dante, he turned his back on the ruckus. "We can go," he stated with a deep sigh. "I did what I came here to do."

Seeing that the bar-backs and bouncers had put an end to the brawl, Dante agreed. Surveying the damage, he could tell the guy would be in need of a few stitches, in the least, if not worse. "Nice work," he complemented, his stiff finger indicating the blood dripping from their victim's face.

"Yeah," Charlie clipped, not willing to voice his pleasure at the deed; however, he didn't have to. The satisfaction he felt at being the judge, jury and executioner of men radiated from every ounce of his being.

FIFTEEN

All in a Day's Work

ARRIVING BACK at the barn well after midnight, Charlie and Dante had decided they would set up the very bombs one of the bald men had been constructing to destroy them. Taking a few of the devices, one was placed in the small shed, ready to detonate. They positioned a few others around the base of the house. Prepared to make their move, the pair curled up in the loft of the barn, which hardly qualified as comfortable, and drifted off to sleep.

Awakened some hours later by the sound of voices, Charlie peered out of the upper level to see about a dozen men moving around below him. "Hey," he called to his partner, "I think they're up t' somethin'."

"Oh yeah?" Dante stretched and got to his feet. "Well, get over to the house and take care of that girl, then. We need to get this done before they can pack up and get out of here."

Quick to obey, Charlie teleported to the top of the stairs inside the house. Surveying the living area below him, he saw no sign of any of the men. Looking into the bedrooms as he came to them, he found them deserted, until he reached the last one. The floor creaked as he entered, and he thought about the kitchen below for an instant before he saw the mass of dark hair and the naked lump of flesh tied to the bed.

"Jesus," he muttered, moving further in to see if she were truly alone.

Studying her, he noted the shallow breaths and felt relieved that they hadn't killed her. *How am I gonna get her out of here?* he pondered for a moment. Deciding it would be better to act as a man rather than a spirit, he quickly crossed the plane and began untying her bonds.

Regaining consciousness, the girl's soft blue eyes stared up at him. "Who the hell are you?" she croaked, pulling her newly freed hand down and lightly touching the bruised and oozing flesh that covered her ribs.

"I'm here to help you," he whispered back. "We gotta hurry. Put your clothes on, and let's get out o' here."

Obediently tugging on her jeans, the girl's face crinkled in pain. Her top had been badly ripped, but she donned the remaining rags. "Where'd they go?" she stammered, pulling the cloth to cover her breasts.

"They're outside. I have a friend with me, an' he's got a little surprise for them, but we can't be in here when it goes off," Charlie handed her shoes over. Watching the curve of flesh escaping from her destroyed tee, he removed his own shirt and gave her that as well.

Accepting the article, she discarded the blood soaked version and pulled his on instead. Shoving her feet into the leather sneakers, the girl pushed a mass of knotted hair out of her eyes and followed him to the door. Staying close behind, the pair crept down the stairs. Peeking into the kitchen, they crossed the empty room hurriedly and glared out the back door.

"I don't see anyone," she hissed.

"No, I think they're all out front," Charlie agreed. "You take off; head into th' trees and then climb t' the top o' the ridge. Get as far away as you can, an' don' stop runnin' for anything." Staring into her blue eyes, he felt reminded of Clarisse, with her pure innocence staring back at him.

"Thank you," she managed quietly, tears welling in her crystal blue orbs.

"Don't mention it," Charlie grasped her arm and gave it a squeeze. "Now go!"

Making her exit, she stomped across the porch and down the steps. Catching the screen door and preventing it from slamming, Charlie shifted back into the other plane, hiding himself from anyone who might enter the kitchen as he watched her go.

When the back of her dark hair disappeared into the foliage, he tele-pathically selected a new shirt from his closet back at Purgatory and transported it to himself, then pulled it over his head. *Being a teleporter has its advantages,* he mused. Again decent, he turned on his heel and headed to the front and out to find his partner.

"She's clear," he informed Dante when he had located him. "You set?"

"Yeah," the leader agreed. "They're having some kind of meeting in the barn, so our timing couldn't be better." An instant later, the pair stood on the top of the ridge, and without hesitating, Dante set off the charges.

The blast rocked the earth beneath them, and a huge fireball shot up from the barn as bits of wood and debris showered the ground around them. "Holy crap!" Charlie exclaimed, watching as a flaming form burst out of the smoke and dropped to the ground in a futile attempt to extin-guish himself.

Seeing the girl reach the top of the incline a few hundred feet away, she only glanced over her shoulder before beginning her descent down the other side. "You think she'll be ok?"

"Yeah, she'll get some help when she gets out to the highway," Dante clamped Charlie on the shoulder. "Good work, by the way. Karma's sure to be pleased," he indicated their inferno below them.

"All in a day's work," Charlie agreed, feeling oddly content with the outcome, despite the carnage. "I guess we head back to Purgatory?"

"Yeah, we've done all we can here," Dante matched his companion's smile. "You did good there, boy. You just might turn out to be all right after all," he teased before they both disappeared, leaving the fire to burn itself out.

Arriving in the dining area a moment later, a room full of Forgotten Angels sat enjoying their typical breakfast feast. Only creating a mild flurry of excitement, the gathering continued with their meal. Taking a plate, Charlie moved to join them, noticing that Phil scowled at him from his seat next to Karma.

"Well done," their mistress congratulated them, shifting to give the man to her right a dark glare. Rising, Phil moved into the empty chair next to him, vacating the spot so that Charlie and Dante could each sit beside her. "You made that look easy."

"It was easy," Charlie agreed, digging into his scrambled eggs eagerly. "I think I'm getting used to this *dispenser of justice* gig."

"Indeed you are, and rightly so," she leaned against her hands, elbows planted in front of her. "Giving her the shirt off your back was a nice touch, by the way," she praised. Glancing at Dante, she smiled. "You work well together and have earned a bit of reward."

Seeing the look pass between them, Charlie chuckled, "He can have th' reward. I'm jus' glad it's over."

"Really," Karma shifted her gaze to him. "I was thinking of getting you something special. Something you've longed to have."

Pausing in mid bite, he hesitated a moment before he breathed quietly, "Are you serious?" His mind racing, he could only think of one thing, the only thing, he longed for. "You're going to get her for me?"

"Yes, I have arranged for her release," Karma beamed. "She will arrive this evening, and she will be yours." She paused, adjusting her plate for a moment before it disappeared. "Of course, we had to make a concession to achieve the deal, and Gous will also be freed."

"Gous," Charlie's brown eyes darkened and he grunted, "Well, that's great. So I'll have him t' contend with again."

"Not that it matters," Karma reassured him. "You are stronger now, and he will think twice before confronting you."

Realizing that she was correct, Charlie grinned at the idea of turning the tables on the Dark Angel. "Oh, yeah! I can cross the plane now, an' he doesn't hold all the cards."

"Exactly," Dante raised his cup of coffee in a mock toast. He had warmed to the new-comer over the course of their mission, whether he had intended it or not. Grinning at Charlie, he took a sip, and then addressed the female between them, "So, when do I get my prize?"

"Oh, as soon as you finish your breakfast, baby," she cooed. "Everyone gets what they deserve when Karma's around."

SIXTEEN

Date with an Angel

CHARLIE ANXIOUSLY STARED out the window, watching the desert sun set. He had spent the day preparing his surprises for Clarisse and now stood in the atrium, awaiting her arrival. *Things sure have changed,* he lamented to himself. He thought of the last time he had set up a special day for a girl; *Tabitha.* That day had ended badly, and he had driven his guardian away because of it.

Not today, he promised himself. *Today, I have a date with an angel.* Things would be decidedly different, and he would have eternity to demonstrate his love for her.

It had been over a year since he had seen her. She had been Donna then; the girl he wanted to marry. Shoving his hand into his pocket, he toyed with the box he had retrieved that morning, contemplating the jeweled band hidden inside it. *Thank God I kept it,* he grinned. If everything went well, he intended to give it to her; *the love of my life.*

Sensing a presence, he turned, his eyes scanning the room. Seeing nothing, he shifted to the other plane and presented himself to her shyly, "Hello, beautiful."

Clarisse's wide blue eyes glistened, "Charlie?" Her voice soft, her bewilderment at his appearance in her world evident, she gasped, "How?"

Next to her in an instant, he placed his hands firmly on her hips, his lips caressing hers before moving to her cheek as he whispered, "I'll explain, but not now. I jus' wanna hold you, love."

Leaning against him, she exhaled a deep sigh, and a moment later, bright morning light shone around them. Feeling the sand beneath her feet, she could hear the crash of the waves surrounding them.

Releasing her, Charlie revealed their destination; a secret love nest on a deserted island. "Do you like it?" he asked, indicating the canopy covered bed in the center of the beach.

The wind rustled the chiffon curtains that served as walls, and her long pale fingers caught the fine material. Awed by the detail, she stepped onto the platform and admired the pillows and thick, fluffy comforter that adorned the mattress. A small table stood next to it, a bottle of wine in a bucket of ice and two glasses in the center of it.

"You thought of everything," she breathed, turning to face the sea. Inhaling the salty air, peace settle over her. "How long do we have?"

"Forever," he replied, his hands moving around her torso to embrace her from behind. Her flesh warm beneath her thin white gown, he caressed her. Nuzzling her neck, he located the curve of her jaw, his lips and tongue dotting the line of it with soft kisses.

The girl shivered, feeling him to the depths of her being. Turning to face him, she admitted quietly. "I've never... not as me. Not as Clarisse."

"It's ok," he toyed with her ear, his fingers brushing her long blond strands aside. "I loved you as Donna and I love you as Clarisse. You are one and the same, the half that makes me whole." He smiled, prepared to bare his soul, "I've missed you so much; waited every day to be with you again." With his free hand, he presented the velvet covered box. "Will you marry me?"

Her jaw trembled, her lips parting in awe when he opened the lid to expose his offering. "Oh, Charlie!"

The sea breeze rustling his hair, he waited for her reply. *Just breathe,* he reminded himself for the umpteenth time that day. He wanted her so desperately, he couldn't fathom her refusal.

After a long pause, she gazed into his eyes. Almost the same height, she matched him squarely, "I'm not sure that Destiny would allow it."

"It doesn't matter," he grinned, "Destiny doesn't own you anymore. Things are different, love. Say yes; I know you want to. Follow your heart an' damn the consequences."

Squinting against the whiffs of hair that floated around her, she nodded, "You really think I can do that?"

"Yeah, you can do that," he chuckled back at her. "Baby, we were made for each other. Trust me. Let me put this ring on your finger," he shifted playfully, "An' put you in that bed as my wife."

Laughing with him, joy sprang up from deep inside her; like a well of hope that could not be squelched. "Ok," she agreed, stepping back, "But how are we going to be married here in the middle of nowhere?"

Instantly, Dante stood on the sand beneath them, looking official in a white suit and tie. "You have need of a minister?" he sang pleasantly.

Her eyes darting quickly between them, she giggled, "You thought of everything."

"Yes," Charlie took her hand and guided her to a small platform that awaited them a few yards down the beach. Dancing shade from the towering trees protected the wooden floor, and a table prepared for a ceremony sat in the middle of it. Taking a knee, he knelt on one of the white satin pillows and indicated for her to join him on the other.

"Oh, sweet Destiny," she whispered, pulling at her gown to maneuver herself into proper position.

Standing before the couple, Dante administered the rights, referring to an ancient text periodically. His voice warm, he divined that their union be blessed by the power of the ancient beings. Pouring a generous amount of red wine into a large crystal goblet, he presented it to each of them to drink. "So shall you share in the cup of life," he announced.

With one hand on each of their heads, the power of his being radiated around them. "Place the ring on her finger," he instructed.

Doing as he requested, Charlie held her trembling digit and slid the tip through the golden band. Working it down to the base of her finger, he sniffed, blinking back his tears. Looking her in the eye, he could see she had given up on fighting hers, and droplets of joy glistened on her cheeks.

"By the power of the Light and the Dark, may you be joined for eternity," Dante concluded his ritual. "You should kiss your bride."

Leaning towards her, Charlie didn't hesitate, tasting her fully before his hand caught her jaw. His fingers caressing her lips, he whispered, "Hello, Mrs. Phillips."

Grinning, she eagerly agreed, "I can't believe this is real. I'm so happy, Charlie."

Clamping his friend on the shoulder, Dante announced loudly, "I'm off. You two enjoy yourselves, and I'll see you in Purgatory."

"Purgatory?" her eyes grew wide as their companion disappeared.

"Forget it," Charlie got to his feet, helping her to hers. "All that can wait. Right now, we have love t' make." Lifting her into his arms, he carried her across the sand and placed her onto the pliable surface. Her gown gone in the blink of an eye, she lay before him in all her naked splendor.

Dispensing with his own clothing, he hung over her, drinking in the cool blue of her eyes and tantalizing his digits with the feel of her bare flesh. "I love you," he informed her softly.

"I know," she replied, her fingers finding their way through his brown waves to his scalp. "Oh Charlie, I love you, too!"

His lips suctioning to hers in small kisses, he pressed against her and the feel of her set his body ablaze.

SEVENTEEN

The Price We Pay

TWISTING in the bed and pouring a glass of wine for each of them, Charlie smiled at the sun sinking into the bay before them. "Did I get it right?" he indicated their surroundings. Handing her a crystal goblet, he nestled back into the rich covers and took a sip of his own.

"Very right," she agreed, her long frame lying next to his. "It's beautiful, Charlie. Thank you."

Swirling the dark liquid, he lay his arm behind her shoulders, pulling her tighter against him. "I have things to tell you," he said quietly. "I'm not sure they can wait."

"I know," she agreed, unwilling to disturb their love-nest by moving. "I'm ready. Together, we can face it, whatever it is."

"I hope so," he agreed, then began in earnest. "Have you ever heard of Karma?"

"Karma?" she repeated, turning the name over in her mind for a moment. "No; should I have?"

"She's the twins' mother; Destiny and Fate. Keeper's mate."

"Charlie!" Clarisse bolted straight up, almost spilling their glasses. The blankets falling around her waist, her perfect breasts commanded his attention before she pulled the sheet up to cover them. "How dare you speak of Keeper so casually!" she rebuked.

Taking her glass from her firm grasp, he placed them both on the table next to the bed. "Let's move," he implored. "I think this's gonna be difficult for you, an' I want you t' be comfortable when I explain about the price we pay for the lives we lead."

"The price we pay?" she repeated in confusion. "Charlie, just tell me!"

Looking into her soft blue orbs, he returned her clothing to her thin frame, dressing her in the gown he loved to see flowing about her. Whisking them down the beach, he placed her on a blanket and knelt beside her, donning his own simple jeans and tee. Staring at the white foam glistening in the last light of the day, he sighed. "Baby, you only ever heard half the story; half the truth. Keeper's half."

Clenching her jaw, Clarisse bit back a sharp reply. Instead, she managed a calm response, "Ok, let's pretend for a moment that you are correct. Keeper is the protector of balance. He makes the world safe."

Shaking his head, Charlie sighed. "Yes, he does keep the balance. He and Karma created the twins to ensure that neither side would take control. That's what happened in their world; that's why they came here. We are their second chance to get it right."

Looking her in the eye, he waited. She stared back at him, unsure if she should speak. When he said nothing else, she asked submissively, "All right, where did they come from?"

"I don' know," he admitted. "I only know it wasn't here. Karma came t' get me an' kept the judge from sending me t' prison. After I got t' Purgatory, she revealed that much t' me; then she started trainin' me."

"Training you," she dropped his gaze, turning her attention to the calming effect of the sea, "To do what?"

"Karma is the dispenser of justice," he supplied quietly. "She sends us on missions, kind o' like the Summer Angels, but not really. We don' have clients; we get assigned targets. People who have somethin' comin' t' them. We make sure they get whatever that is."

"You punish people," she concluded, her voice hollow as she stared straight ahead.

"Yeah," he brushed at a few grains of sand on the blanket next to him. "Look -" he began before she cut him off.

"You're a Dark Angel."

"No!" he shouted, disturbed by the comparison. "We're Forgotten Angels, that's what we are! We aren't light, an' we ain't dark. We don't manipulate people. We don' save them or any o' that. We make sure they get whatever it is that they have earned," he simplified for her.

Turning to stare at him, she demanded, "Why would you choose to do this? Why would you go against Keeper like this?' her voice caught, aware that he had dragged her into his choice and made her a part of his crime.

"Baby, don't cry," he soothed, brushing her cheek gently before he kissed her moist skin. "It's not like that. When I joined the rest of Karma's minions, she promised me that we would be together. Did Keeper give us that? Did he even care that we were in love?" his voice grew bitter. "Hell no, he didn't!"

"Charlie, don't!" she breathed.

"Don't *Charlie, don't,* me!" he growled back. "Listen t' me. This is where we belong. This is the side we were meant t' take. Why do you think Destiny an' Keeper – an' Father! None o' them ever told you the truth; none o' them ever mentioned Karma. Why do you think that is?" he scowled.

Blinking at him rapidly, she considered their reasons. Coming up with nothing, she asked quietly, "Why then? Why would they not tell us? I was a Light Angel, Charlie! A Summer Angel, and it was my job to take care of my clients!"

"You were a pawn, baby," he consoled. "They used the goodness inside your heart and gave you a job that served their purpose. They don' care about humans; they need us, plain and simple."

"Need us for what?" she begged, her thoughts clouded by the pain of betrayal.

"I don' know that," he sighed, pulling his knees up to lean on. "Not yet, at least. I'm gonna find out, though," he promised. "Stay with me baby. Follow my lead. Together, we are strong, an' I need you by my side."

Seeing the truth shining in his mahogany eyes, she could not deny him. Clarisse had been lost in Charles Phillips since he was a boy.

Watching him grow had become her obsession, and she had once put distance between them to stop the feelings that made her feel guilty. "I have loved you for so long," she whispered.

"I know; I've always known," he replied, planting a small kiss on her lips. "You're mine, love. Body an' soul."

"Do you have any idea what this is going to cost us?" she persisted.

"Everyone has t' take a side," he agreed. "Everyone must choose, an' there is always a price to be paid, either way. Taking Keeper's side would have cost me you, an' that's something I wasn't prepared t' lose. Please," he paused, searching her crystal blue orbs. "Please forgive me, Clarisse. I had to do this. I couldn't face eternity without you."

EIGHTEEN

The Way We Were

TAKING CHARLIE'S HAND, Clarisse whisked them away from their secluded honeymoon suite. Standing in bright sunlight, he grimaced, aware that she was prepared to put up a fight over his choice. Sighing loudly, he waited for her to make her case, certain it was too late and he couldn't change his mind, even if he wanted to.

A few minutes later, a couple came along on the path next to them, swinging a toddler between them. The little girl giggled loudly, holding her parents' hands as she bounced along, putting her feet down for a few steps before she leapt again and they caught her in a slow swooping motion.

"Do you recognize them?" Clarisse asked quietly, unsure if his memory of their visit to that location had returned.

"No," he clipped in an irritated tone.

"They were my clients. Last time we were here, their daughter was an infant; Father saved them from a Dark Angel," she informed him quietly.

Recalling the dream that had revealed the scene to him, Charlie rocked his jaw side to side. "Look, I realize that you were emotionally invested in your clients. I'm not sayin' you're wrong. All I'm sayin' is, you didn' know the whole story."

"But I helped them, Charlie. That's enough for me. My life had a purpose. I protected them," she sighed. "It was noble and just."

"Ok," he wobbled his head around, then agreed, "You did a great job of taking care of them; I'll be the first t' admit that. But you have t' understand -"

She cut him off again, squeezing his hand and transporting them to a large fenced yard, filled with headstones. The sky pitch black above them, wind rustled in the trees, their leaves shading them from the light of the moon.

"Shit," he murmured under his breath, and he knew he couldn't win. He couldn't fight a hundred years of indoctrination; she had too much invested in the other side to ever see reason. "I'm sorry, baby," he whispered. "So who's this?"

"Another of my clients," she indicated the grave before them. "The Dark Angels took him; Gous took him."

"The beggar," Charlie breathed.

Her face jerking to stare at him, she accused, "You do remember!"

"I have dreams," he confessed. "I remember things. I'm not sure how much, but yeah; I remember this guy." He met her gaze, shame on his face. "This doesn't change anything," he sighed. "Don't you get it? We have to figure this out. All of this," he swung his hands out, dropping her digits and stepping back to indicate their surroundings. "All of this is staged. It's fake. Neither side is going to win because both sides are using us. Destiny and Fate; they're not fighting over us."

"Yes, they are," Clarisse stamped her foot in disgust.

"No, baby; they're not," he inched towards her, framing her face in his palms. "Keeper wants balance. The twins work for him, an' that's all there will ever be. Both sides suffering in their sick game."

"And what do you suggest we do about it? You want to take this Karma's side? To follow her? What makes her so great?" Clarisse demanded, wiping at an escaped tear.

"I told you, I'm not sure how or why, but Karma's working against Keeper. She wants t' stop the twins. She helped put all o' this in motion, but something happened," he dropped his hands to his sides, releasing her. "She wants to put an end to what they created."

"She told you that? She said she wants to destroy it all?"

"No, not in so many words," he confessed, feeling chilled in the evening air. "Let's go back to our beach," he implored.

"No," she shook her head in disgust. "I have a few more things to show you."

"No," he almost screamed, feeling the anger rising inside him. "I don't need to see any more. I know how it was; I know who and what you were. But those days an' that life are gone." His eyes glowed with a soft green hue. "I'm not a Dark Angel, and I would never hurt you. But I cannot allow you to interfere, either."

Staring at him, her heart raced. "Charlie, what's happened to you?"

"I told you. I'm a Forgotten Angel; minion of Karma. I ensure that people get what they deserve. Exactly what they deserve," he changed his wardrobe and covered himself with a dark jacket. "I have powers, Clarisse. Better and greater than you can imagine."

"Oh, Charlie," she breathed, fear twisting her gut.

"I don't wanna force you. Please, don't make me…"

Sucking in a ragged breath, tears streaked down her cheeks. "It was such a beautiful day."

"It still is," he replied more gently, "Or it can be. You jus' have t' see reason. You have t' understand that the way things were wasn't real. You have t' accept that the truth is now before you. You have to be willing t' take your place among the Forgotten Angels."

NINETEEN

Father's Promise

"CHARLIE," a deep male voice cut through the darkness, seeming to echo off the stone markers.

Stiff, the young man cast his gaze around him. "Who's there?" he shouted, half afraid that Keeper had come for him, and he would soon discover how strong his powers really were.

Moving into the moonlight, a rounded figure in a flowing white robe stood before him. Pointing at the long white beard, Charlie accused, "You."

"Father!" Clarisse squealed, throwing herself against the shorter man and hugging him tightly. "I'm so glad you found us!"

"Easy my child," the elder Summer Angel pushed at her thin frame, backing her away. Turning his attention to the young man, he nodded. "Special you are. I've said it before. And in league with Karma, no less."

"You know about her?" Clarisse gasped, taken aback that Charlie had been right on at least that account.

"Yes," Father began to pace a small area of dirt. "I know about her."

"You're not really human, are you," Charlie accused, certain every step moved them closer to the truth. "How many others of your kind came here with Karma and Keeper?"

"Careful, Charlie," Father warned. "Your curiosity has gotten you into trouble before."

"Stow it," he retorted angrily, "I'm tired of your games. I want answers."

"Well, what makes you think you are entitled to answers, hmm?" Father ended the pacing and faced him squarely. "You and your generation. Always feeling you are entitled. That's what's wrong with this world."

The air caught in Charlie's chest. *What's wrong with this world,* he breathed to himself.

Father could see the idea spark in the eyes of his adversary. "Smart man, Charlie Phillips."

Aware that the two of them had shared a silent connection, Clarisse demanded loudly, "What's going on? What are you talking about?"

"Charlie knows," Father chuckled. "I am not one of them," he continued in his raspy old voice. "But I did discover their secrets, many centuries ago."

"Do tell," Charlie quipped.

"When the time is right, you will discern what you are intended to know. I am not here to set your mind at ease," Father replied calmly, pivoting slowly to face the girl.

Stricken with terror, Clarisse froze. Feeling the anguish to the tips of her toes, she gasped, "Please, Father. Tell me it is not so."

"Clarisse, you are a woman of many years. A child you were, when you came from the waters of the Atlantic. Taken in by Destiny and given a purpose, you have lived in the shadow of a dark secret. One that Charlie has only begun to discover," he replied cryptically.

"Yeah, more riddles," Charlie blurted. Turning his palms up, he demanded firmly, "Don' you people ever jus' say what you mean?"

Giving him a brief scowl, Father remained focused on the girl, "Put your mind at ease, my daughter. Follow your heart and have faith in your mate."

Stunned, Charlie recovered quickly, "Yeah, wife. Listen t' your old man," he translated loosely.

Her eyes flicking between them, Clarisse briefly considered if Father had somehow been taken in by Karma. Could she trust the man she had looked up to for so many decades? "How do I know you speak the truth?" she challenged.

"I make you no promises, Summer Angel; save one. The universe is a vast void, made smaller in the arms of the one who loves you." With a wave of his hand, the old man disappeared, leaving the couple in surprised silence.

Minutes ticked by. The wind rustled the trees above them, causing the shadows to dance around them in the quiet of the dead.

"What the hell was that all about?" Charlie eventually spoke first.

"I have no idea," Clarisse breathed deeply, "but I think he was trying to convince me to follow you."

"Yeah," her mate nodded. "That part I got."

Cutting her eyes over at her new husband, the girl felt a flutter of joy in her gut. Giggling at his surliness, she grinned, "Should I take the old codger's advice?"

A slow smile spread across Charlie's lips, "You most certainly should." Offering her his hand, he waited for her to come to him.

Moving slowly, as if unsure about her choice, Clarisse inched towards him. "What if he's wrong? What if you're wrong?"

"I can't be right all the time," Charlie countered, playfully curling his fingers at her before she took his hand. "See, that's better," he squeezed her digits. "We're a team, and there's nothin' I wouldn' do for you."

Sliding into his arms, she relaxed against his chest. Taken with the urge to make love to him, she transported them back to the darkness of their island paradise.

Finding that the air had grown cold there as well, with the ocean breeze blowing in on them, Charlie set fire to a large pit filled with wood at the head of their bed; bathing their bodies in warm orange glow. Sliding her robe off her shoulder and dropping it to the floor, he growled, "You tempt me so deeply, earth woman."

Biting her lip, she sighed. "I love you, Charlie. I'm really scared of what all of this means."

"Don't be scared," he toyed with her skin, dragging his fingers lightly across it before removing his own clothing with only a thought. Turning and pushing her across the thick comforter, he clasped her hands and lay them over her head. Holding her in place, he parted her legs with his own and claimed her prize.

"We're gonna do this every night," he whispered against her ear.

"Oh, Charlie," she replied, wrapping herself around him, drawing him deeper inside her.

TWENTY

Fighting Fire

THE FIRE HAD BURNED itself out when Charlie awoke the following morning. Opening one eye and then the other, the bright light of mid-day greeted him warmly. Lying still, the sea breeze stirred the translucent material that surrounded them. The shallow breaths of the woman pressed against him put an ache in his chest.

Deep down, he knew that he was right about Karma. He only hoped that Clarisse had been, or would be, convinced, and that no trouble would come from her presence in Purgatory. His benefactor had promised that the girl would be his, and in fact she was. However, she had neglected to stipulate for how long, and he feared that once again their days together were numbered.

Stricken with grief, Charlie recalled the day Donna had ended her own life, essentially taking Clarisse with her; or vice versa. When speaking of a body inhabited by a ghost, it's hard to say exactly who is in charge of what. Shifting so he could look squarely at her sleeping form, he traced the line of her jaw with a gentle caress.

"I promise," he whispered against her cheek, "no matter what happens, you and I will never be apart again."

Shifting slightly beneath the weight of him, Clarisse groaned.

Rubbing her shoulder more firmly, he coerced her to consciousness. "Baby," he called softly. "It's time to go home."

"Home," she repeated groggily. Clarisse had not had a home in the true sense of the word in over a century, not counting the few months she had spent in Donna's body. Opening her eyes, she licked her lips, then sat up and pushed her long blond strands out of her face. "Wow."

"This is our place," he informed her, getting to his feet and putting on his clothes casually. "We'll come back here whenever we can."

"I hope so," she agreed, then stood next to him, instantly dressed in white shorts and a tank top, with white canvas sneakers on her feet. "Ok, let's get this over with. I take it Purgatory is Karma's domain?"

"Yeah," he agreed, folding her into his arms. "Jus' relax, and don' piss her off. She can be a real bitch when you get on her bad side," he warned.

"Then I will remain silent," Clarisse agreed.

Staring into her soft blue eyes, Charlie considered what would happen when they got there. Deciding it only fair to warn her, he replied, "She can read your thoughts, love."

Appearing unmoved, she only nodded, "I'm not surprised. Keeper and the twins can, too."

Stunned, Charlie gaped at her, "They can? Why didn't I know that?"

"Because it's rude to read another person's thoughts," she bit curtly. "They have manners; and restraint."

"Oh," he agreed, glancing around them. "Well, Karma's probably going to be poking around inside your head, so be ready for it. Jus' relax and think positive thoughts."

"I will, Charlie," she agreed with a firm nod. "I have chosen you. I won't mess this up for us."

Nodding his understanding, he gripped her more firmly, then transported them to the room where they had met the day before. Releasing her once they had arrived, he looked around to discover the house seemed deserted.

"This is where we were yesterday," she observed, moving away from him.

"Yeah, this is the atrium," he supplied. "The whole place is called Purgatory, an' that," he indicated the barn, "is Karma's private space."

Glancing around, she noticed the tables in the next room. Feeling her stomach rumble, she gasped when a meal appeared on one of the long flat surfaces. Her mouth agape, she moved towards the feast, drawing in the scent of roasted chicken with dressing and vegetables.

"That smells delicious," she breathed. She had gotten used to modern food while parading around as Donna, but had not needed a meal since returning to the plane of the Angels.

She found it curious that those in Purgatory ate real food, like ordinary people, recalling that Charlie had once referred to himself as a hybrid. And she had slept as well; she never needed it while she had been a Summer Angel, and a moment of fear twisted in her gut that she had in fact been altered somehow by her union with him.

"I'm sure that it is," Charlie agreed, retrieving plates for them. "Karma's an excellent cook."

"She did this?" Clarisse leaned over to inhale the aroma more deeply.

"Of course," a female voice interrupted them. Approaching the couple, her red pantsuit scraped noisily as her thighs brushed past each other in time with her heels clicking on the floor. "Hello, Clarisse. I'm Karma Kapoor," the shorter woman extended her hand, her feet and legs falling silent when she stopped before her.

Taking the hand anxiously, Clarisse shook it, her eyes darting over to Charlie for approval. Opening her mouth to speak, her thoughts betrayed her an instant before she realized holding her tongue had done her little good; *damn*.

A slow smile spread across Karma's face as she dropped the appendage. "I like her, Charlie," she informed her minion. "You have chosen well." Lifting a plate, she served herself and assumed her usual seat at the head of the table.

"Where are the others?" Charlie asked, doing the same and taking the chair to her right.

"We will be dining alone today," Karma replied calmly, watching the girl as she selected her food and took the chair to her left, facing her mate. "So tell me," she asked in an excited voice, "What's it like to finally learn about Keeper's dirty little secret?"

Her eyes wide in surprise, Clarisse faltered, "Whatever do you mean?"

"I mean me, of course," Karma grinned, taking a few bites of her meal. "I'm sure it must have come as a shock to learn of my existence."

"Well," Clarisse glared at Charlie, her eyes silently begging for help. When he made no attempt to rescue her, she drew a deep breath and admitted loudly, "Yes, it was a bit of a surprise. No one had ever spoken of you."

"And rightly so," Karma laughed. "But you are beyond that now, and the truth shall set you free."

Anxiously considering what truth Karma might be referring to, Clarisse ate hungrily at her meal. Focusing on keeping her mind on the food, random images of the previous day and night floated in and out of her conscious thought.

Finishing her own, Karma turned to Charlie, "So, you had a visit from Father. How is he?"

"You know Father?" he gasped, scarcely stunned by the revelation. He could feel the secrets being revealed to him, and relished in the idea of gathering more about his benefactor and her people.

"Of course," Karma's laughter tinkled lightly. "I know all of the Light Angels," she cut her eyes over at Clarisse, "And the Dark ones."

"Father is a Summer Angel," Clarisse clarified quickly.

"Yes, of course he is," the woman in charge agreed. "Did he have anything important to share?"

"He told me I should follow Charlie's wishes," Clarisse didn't bother to attempt deception. Karma would have the truth, either way.

"Bright girl," the darker haired woman praised. Turning her attention back to Charlie, she smiled sweetly at him. "You know we should fight fire with fire," she announced.

"What's that supposed to mean?" he replied calmly, disposing of his own empty plate.

"Oh, I don't know," Karma toyed with him, grinning deviously. Tempted to delve into his thoughts, she curled her fists for a moment before scouring the mind of the girl more fully instead. Locating the remnants of their greedy encounters, she sighed, "After having experienced the joining of our spirits, I'm surprised you would find such a coupling satisfying."

Clarisse glared at him for a moment before dropping her gaze back to her unfinished meal. Her hunger removed by the statement, she swallowed before she mumbled, "How do I stop you from stealing my thoughts?" Raising her eyes to meet the warm brown orbs of the woman next to her, she continued a bit more forcefully, "He chose me to be his mate. We are in love, and we don't need your meddling in our lives."

Studying her, Karma leaned back in her seat. "Perfect. Charlie, I have to hand it to you. She's better than any I could have chosen."

"I don't understand," he admitted quietly, relieved that Clarisse hadn't been struck down on the spot for insubordination.

"No, I don't suppose that you do," Karma agreed. Folding her hands in front of her, the look of contentment on her face gave Charlie a sick feeling in the pit of his gut. "You have always been special. Keeper wanted you for his cause, but I have claimed his prize. You have become a trusted member of my house, and you have brought a Summer Angel to join us." Sensing the distress of the young woman to her left she addressed her instead.

"I feel your passion. I sense your devotion to your mate. Stronger than even the ties that once held Keeper and I as one. Call yourself what you will, you are part of us. And I have a special task for you."

Glaring at her, Clarisse could not believe her ears. "I'm not one of your minions," she bit angrily at the absurd suggestion. Leaping to her feet, she stammered, "I think I've made a mistake coming here."

"A mistake?" Karma breathed, her eyes growing lighter, "The only mistake would be to think that you could ever leave. That you could defy me. When I say there is a task for you, you will take it. And you will complete it."

Glancing at the man seated next to her, her eyes paled to misty green. His body stiff, Charlie stood for a moment before collapsing to the floor. "See my puppet?" the auburn haired beauty breathed. "He does my bidding for you," she informed her newest recruit curtly. "Should you choose to try my patience, it would be he who would taste my sting."

"Stop it!" Clarisse squealed, darting around the empty seats and dropping to her knees beside him. His eyes wide and unseeing, he stared past her, into the oblivion that surrounded them. "Stop, please!"

"Swear to me," Karma hissed, rising slowly, a red gown flowing around her. "Pledge to me and to him that you will serve us."

"I can't," the girl cried, touching his face, the coolness of his flesh unnerving her. "Destiny, please!"

"She cannot help you here. This is my home; the part of this planet granted to me on our arrival. None of our kind may set foot here without my welcome; not even you, Clarisse."

Brushing his hair back, tears dripped from her blue eyes. "Please, Karma," she begged more quietly. "Please don't take him from me."

"I need your word," Karma insisted calmly.

Gripping his tee-shirt, then rubbing his chest, Clarisse could feel no sign of breath, no indication of life. Her mind drawn rapidly to the fight with Gous, when Charlie had pledged himself to be her guardian angel, she recalled that it had been Keeper who had preserved his life. *And now Karma is going to take it.*

"Foolish girl! You think I want to destroy him?" Karma's voice boomed.

"I can't," Clarisse cried, tears staining her cheeks. "Don't you see? I can't betray them, not even to save Charlie!"

"Then you will both die," Karma pursed her lips angrily.

"Wait!" Dante stepped into the room, "Wait," he stated again more calmly. "She just got here," he indicated the fair haired girl kneeling over his new friend. Staring at his governess, he conveyed his plan to her silently.

Blinking a few times, Karma smiled, imparting her reply; "*You think it will work?*"

"*Doesn't matter, it's worth a shot,*" he replied in kind. "Free him," he said aloud. "I will vouch for them; both of them," he smiled down at Clarisse.

Recognizing him from their joining, she gasped, "You're Charlie's friend!"

"Yes," he knelt next to the other male, relieved when he started to sputter and cough for air. Helping him to sit up, he clapped him on the back a few times, "Come on, buddy; don't quit on me now."

TWENTY-ONE

Set Things Straight

"I CAN'T BELIEVE she nearly killed me," Charlie lamented, he eyes fixed on the roll of the waves in the distance.

Clarisse sniffed loudly, sitting in the sand next to him on their beach. Pulling her white blanket around her more snugly, she sighed, "I think that she would have, had it not been for Dante."

"No doubt," the second man agreed, his golden spikes glistening as he removed his clothing and stretched out to bathe in the sun and deepen his golden flesh.

Watching him, Clarisse considered the life giving rays that once had restored her energy. "I'm not a Summer Angel any more, am I?" she quietly inquired.

"No, you're not," Dante shaded his eyes for a moment to look at her before lying back and closing them again. "You two need to relax."

"How can I relax?" Charlie demanded curtly. "I've made a mistake, and my choice to follow Karma was wrong."

"Right or wrong doesn't matter," his cohort disagreed. "The choice is made, and you will be rewarded for your devotion. That's how Karma is; with her, you always get what you deserve."

"Not always," Charlie shook his head slowly, then shifted to drop his arm around Clarisse's shoulders. "She would have killed me; us. Because we wouldn't do what she wanted."

Laughing loudly, Dante sat up, addressing the couple more firmly, "Man, don't you get it? If you hadn't agreed and done what she wanted, then that's *exactly* what you would have deserved, from her point of view. That's Karma just being herself."

Blinking a few times, Clarisse nodded slowly. "I guess I see your point. So, what do we do from here?"

"We have to set things straight," Dante stood and dusted the sand from his flesh. "You have to prove you are one of the Forgotten Angels; Karma's minion and follower. Charlie's already demonstrated his ability and will to follow her. Unless he really screws up, he's got it made. Now, it's your turn."

Inhaling sharply, Clarisse cut her eyes over at her mate. "What does he mean... that you've proven yourself, and demonstrated your ability?"

Not meeting her gaze, Charlie pulled his arm away and tossed small shells from the shore into the lapping ebb and flow. "I've done what I had to do," he informed her. "I can't say that I don' like it, either. Because I do," he raised his chin to glare at her. "It makes me feel powerful, holdin' a man's fate in my hands."

"Oh, Charlie," she signed, her blue orbs filled with sorrow. "No one controls such things; Fate owns the future of men."

"No," he shook his head. "I own it. I am the dispenser of justice. Good or bad, I see to it that people get what's comin' t' them," he thumped his chest for emphasis. The breeze blew against them, and she shivered.

"Nice to see you finally on the right path," a deep voice called on the wind.

Instantly stiff, Charlie and Clarisse both looked around wildly, and Dante froze and then whispered, "Who's that?"

"Gous," Charlie growled, "All right, show yourself, Dark Angel." He felt annoyed that events had been progressing downhill rapidly.

"My pleasure," Gous appeared next to Dante, and Charlie leapt up to square off with his arch rival.

Struggling to find her feet, Clarisse whined loudly, "We aren't going to have any fighting. I have had it!"

"Oh, angry now, are we?" Gous hissed. "Thought you were being smart refusing my proposal all these years. And look where it has gotten you."

Her eyes flashed, and she clutched her cover more tightly around her. "You… animal! I wouldn't have been any better off if I had joined you!"

Smiling, exposing his pointed teeth, Gous hummed a sweet reply, "We would have made an unbeatable team. Perhaps we still can," he hinted.

"What's that supposed t' mean?" Charlie demanded, positioning himself between them. "Stay behind me," he commanded to her over his shoulder.

"Always the protective one," Gous nodded, shifting his gaze over to Dante. "You should go."

"No," Karma's right hand man stood his ground. "Whatever you're planning, I want in on it."

"In on it?" Charlie gasped. "You can't be serious. We're no match for her! Even together, she would crush us. Besides, you were jus' saying that I'm in her good graces, an' Clarisse needs to prove herself. Why would we screw that up with some stupid plan hatched by an untrustworthy piece of filth?"

Gous and Dante glared at one another, each aware of things the couple that shared the beach had yet to discover. Finally, Dante ended the silence, "There are things that we can do, if we really think taking a stand against her would help. But I'm telling you, we're better off staying on Karma's good side."

"Exactly!" Charlie shouted, taking a step towards the figure before him. The wind whipping the dark robe around his enemy's legs, he put a finger in his face. "Leave. Now. And don't ever come around me or my wife again."

"And you think you can stop me?" Gous' tone grated, as if it were nails dragging across a chalk board.

"I'm not the kid I was last time we met," Charlie informed him, never breaking his ice cold glare. "I'm a minion of Karma and a champion of justice. I am strong t' my core, an' I would have no problem taking you down should you ever get in my way."

Clenching his jaw, the muscles in his neck bulged, his rage hidden just below the surface of his calm exterior. Without giving a reply, the Dark Angel vanished, leaving the trio in stunned silence.

"Unbelievable," Dante exhaled.

"Do you think he's really gone?" Clarisse asked timidly, moving closer so she could press herself against Charlie's back.

Scanning the area, Charlie cut his eyes around them. "He better'd be," he warned. "I wasn' kidding. He so much as hints at trouble in our direction, an' it will be on." Turning to take her in his arms, he silently hoped it wouldn't come to that, and that the three of them would finally have a place that they belonged.

PART III
Karma's Legacy

Prologue

"I CAN'T BELIEVE you're trading rooms," Annalise whined, watching her roommate of more than two years pulling her things out of drawers.

"I have to," Portia replied crisply. "I can't stand being in here with the ghost girl any longer."

Clarisse's eyes grew wide, her mouth falling open in disgust. "I am not a ghost!" she squealed.

"You are to me," Portia bit angrily, not bothering to turn around. She knew there would be nothing there if she did. The disembodied voice gave her an odd feeling in her gut, and she wished the girl had never come to Purgatory and disrupted their lives.

"She's talking to you again," Anna observed more quietly.

"Yes, she never shuts up," Portia complained. "But she likes this room across from Charlie, so you two can share. I'll go where I can have some peace."

"But I can't talk to her," the older woman observed, "Or hear her. What good is a roommate you can't tell is there?" Anna had come to Purgatory almost a decade ago, soon after Dante's arrival, at the age of twenty-five. During her time as one of Karma's minions, she hadn't made any real friends, and Portia being her roommate had been her only companionship. With her gone, her world would be silent and quite lonely.

"We can still be friends," Portia insisted, stuffing her wardrobe into bags for transport. "We'll just do it from down the hall." Taking her belongings, she spun around and walked out, unknowingly passing through Clarisse on her way.

Clarisse watched her go with doleful eyes. Shifting to stare at Annalise, she sniffled. She had come to the house weeks ago, and had been doing her best to fit in, for Charlie's sake. However, being in a separate plane from most of the others had presented a good deal of challenges.

"Chin up," Phil's voice echoed from outside the room.

"Hi, Phil," Clarisse replied, brushing at her droplets of sadness.

"It'll be ok," he reassured.

Moving out to the hall, she spied him leaning against the door frame to one of the bathrooms and observing Portia's transition. "I know," she took a few steps towards him. "I'm getting used to this place and all of you. I never imagined that having living people know of my existence could be possible; Charlie was the first, and now this..." she lamented; her world had been torn to shreds and she felt lost in this strange place and its band of outcasts.

Phil only nodded, aware that those who had visited the magical plane and returned hardly qualified as living. Charlie's description of *Forgotten Angel* suited them best; they only half existed in either world, and didn't really belong anywhere.

"What's going on?" Kari demanded, coming up the stairs noisily.

"Portia moved to the other room," Anna informed him, joining the confab in the hall.

Nodding his understanding, Kari grinned at Phil, aware that he had been the most accepting of their new arrival out of all the older household members. "I am pleased I am not disturbed by her presence," he turned to Annalise. "Her existence here has changed us."

"That's because she proves Charlie was right," Phil sauntered towards them, his voice growing quieter. "The other plane is real, even if none of us can go back to it, or remember it for that matter."

"Yes," Anna agreed, looking around anxiously. "Karma doesn't like us talking about the realm of magic, though."

"Of course not," Phil scoffed, "But I'm not afraid of Karma."

"You are a fool, mate," Kari's smile disappeared. "You stay on her bad side and are punished far too often."

Cutting him a cold glare, the older man growled, "I'm not a dog. I'm here against my will, and I refuse to behave, pretending like I'm enjoying myself."

Kari glanced between the two of them, then rolled his eyes around as if looking for Clarisse. "Either way," he answered softly, "We are all here and welcome our new friend, whether we can see and hear her or not."

TWENTY-TWO

A Good Heart

SITTING at the table next to Charlie, Clarisse ate her morning meal while listening to the others. The group of younger males shared a deep comradery, and she had noticed that Charlie had come to fit in with them quite well. Their laughter rising and falling, she knew that her chair appeared unoccupied to them, and she could have sat in her mate's lap and eaten from his plate, and no one would have known the difference.

"You know, that's kind of weird," Raymond observed, pointing his fork at her half-empty dish.

"What is?" Charlie grinned, knowing what he meant before he voiced the observation.

"Watching her food disappear," Myra finished for her twin brother.

Ray and Myra had been at the house the longest of all the Forgotten Angels. By appearance, Charlie guessed them to be only a few years older than him, but they had been serving Karma for longer than Phil, their oldest member, had even been alive. His mind drifting for a moment, he recalled the morning he had discovered the revelation.

He had taken Ray on a mission only a few weeks after his arrival. The pair of them had transported to a small town in Washington State, and they had no hope of blending in as locals. Instead, they posed as passers-through when they entered the diner and took a seat.

"You enjoy being Karma's Minion," Charlie observed, flipping open his menu to make his selection.

"Well, I should," Raymond chuckled, "I've been handing out punishments and rewards for over seventy years. It's nice to have a purpose in this world," he admitted whole-heartedly.

"Seventy years?" Charlie gasped. "You look so young!" he struggled to keep his voice down, aware that other diners could hear their conversation.

"Yes; a gift from Karma. A reward for being such good servants," his companion grinned. "Me and Myra were born in Mexico. We came to the US illegally to find work, but only found trouble instead."

"Wow," the younger man breathed, "So what happened?"

"We worked on farms, moving with the crops for several years. This was back before technology had taken over everything, and a person could hide more easily. Anyways, I got crossways with one of the other migrants who had been traveling with us. I'm not sure how it all came down; Myra and me were killed, only we didn't stay dead. We met Karma afterwards, and she pulled us out of that life; explained to us why we're so different from our old selves. She took us to work on her estate, as she called it."

Intrigued, Charlie had pushed; "So, she always picks up new Forgotten Angels an' brings them into her clan?"

"No," Raymond's eyes narrowed. "Karma only takes in those she has chosen to serve her. Any who don't meet her standards are destroyed."

Charlie felt as if he'd been punched in the gut. *Destroyed*.

Back in the dining room at Purgatory, the ache in his intestines returned, as if he had learned the detail all over again. Glancing at the empty chair next to him, he felt tempted to shift into the magical plane and join her, but instead observed, "I think you guys are jus' jealous 'cause my girl's so unique."

"She isn't unique," Phil countered, "She's a Summer Angel and doesn't belong here."

Karma cleared her throat loudly, joining them at the head of the table. "Not anymore," she announced to the group. "She has become a part of my house, and you will respect that, Phillip."

Cutting his eyes over at their leader, he lifted his chin slowly and squared his gaze. "Yes ma'am," he eventually acquiesced.

Allowing the subject to drop, Karma handed out the day's assignments. "Charlie, I'll meet you and Dante downstairs after breakfast. Kari, you will take Lorren back to Houston and deal with that little problem we've had brewing there," she paused as she sipped her coffee. Indicating Phil with an extended finger, her bright red nails shining in the morning light, she purred, "Clarisse will take you to Manchester. The two of you will need to spend a few days there, since I have a list of good hearts to reward in the area."

"A few days!" Charlie exclaimed, longing to take the girl to their beach, instead.

Glancing at the young man, Karma smiled behind her cup. "Relax, Charlie. She's yours, but she's going to earn her way, the same as the rest."

Glaring at Phil, his chest heaved. Charlie had never liked the other man; not since the first time they had met, when he and his mother had been making the long trek from Texas to California. "Why can't she take Portia, instead?"

Immediately, the other woman's honey colored head perked up, "No!" Her hazel eyes darting around, Portia recovered, "I mean, I have my own list of tasks." She hadn't said she disliked Clarisse, but her actions spoke for her, leaving everyone aware of the conflict between them.

Karma placed her mug on the table, prepared to speak her mind. "I realize that having Clarisse join us has not been easy. However, she is a part of us now; and we need her. There are things she can do for us that none of the rest of you can accomplish."

Charlie swallowed hard, wishing more than ever that he had shifted into the other plane. *Doing it now wouldn't look right,* he lamented to himself. Grinding his teeth, he waited for the lecture to be completed.

Shaking her auburn locks, Karma smiled, "You will all get used to working with her, I assure you. For now, carry on as you always have." With that, she dismissed the group with a wave of her hand, then transitioning into the other plane, she left her chair visibly empty. "Clarisse," she called gently.

"Yes," the long blond strands hid the girl's face.

"You needn't worry about the others," Karma reassured. "Finish your meal, and Phillip will be ready to leave when you are."

Lifting her eyes to meet the deep brown of Ms. Kapoor's, Clarisse sighed loudly. "I'll do my best." She had grown accustomed to their leader regularly probing her thoughts, and had learned to stem the negative ones, crushing them quickly. *At least she talks to me like a person, rather than forcing her words into head.* She appreciated the gesture.

A short time later, Clarisse and Phil arrived at a library, safely nestled between tall shelves of books that masked their unusual mode of transportation.

"Thanks," Phil grinned, whispering to his partner.

"Any time," Clarisse smiled, even though he could not see her face. They had been out on several missions together, and she sensed that he liked her, despite his grouchy demeanor.

Walking through the rows of books, Phil located his target and sauntered over to the table. Taking a seat, he began to work his magic on the human male before him. An empath, he could tell his subject was receptive to his suggestions and quickly became immersed in his task.

Observing quietly from nearby, the blonde smiled genuinely. This was not the work of a guardian angel, by any means. However, she had come to find her tasks with Phil fulfilling in their own way. The boy had done something positive and would be given a favor that would reinforce the action. *I'm still doing good for others,* she sighed to herself; *that's all that matters.*

While she waited, the temptation became too great. Opening her hand flat before her, she produced her seeker, and peered into it cautiously. She had been surprised to discover that she still possessed the device after being released from Keeper's prison. She had only been locked away for a few months, but it had seemed like an eternity that she had spent in the small box, surrounded by darkness.

Scrolling through the screens, she could see her clients and observe them from afar. None had been assigned a new guardian, and she felt forlorn that they faced life without the protection of a guiding hand. She longed to whisk herself away to make an adjustment for them from time to time, but knew that doing so would get her into trouble. Karma had not mentioned the seeker, but Clarisse felt certain she knew of its existence. *Besides, if I abuse it, Destiny may reclaim it.*

The girl might not be able to help her previous charges, but at least being able to observe them brought some sense of peace. The fear of losing the tenuous connection was enough to keep her in line.

Closing her hand when Phil rose from the chair, she said aloud, "Where to next?" Only her partner could hear her voice, and those who sat at the tables and moved silently about the vast room carried on indifferently.

Taking a stroll through the shelves, he located a secluded spot before he replied. "That went well. Next I'd like to visit a couple in Boston."

Transporting them dutifully, Clarisse played her part, sharing her role in their duo without complaint. The day passed quickly, and by late afternoon, they had accomplished all of the tasks that had been laid before them for the day. "Well, I guess we could slip back to Purgatory for the night."

"No," Phil glanced at his watch, then walked casually down the street. To passers-by, he might have appeared to be talking to himself, since his companion remained unseen, but he didn't care. "We have another task late this evening, and I need to watch for a bit before I decide what to do about it."

"Ok," she shrugged, relaxed in his company. "You want to locate something to eat?" They could have gone home to Purgatory, but there would be little point. Charlie would be away on his own missions, and dining in the company of the others held little appeal.

"Sure," he grinned, wishing he could see the girl who toted him about, having grown genuinely fond of Charlie's mate and her lilting voice. "We need to be discreet, though. Can't have people watching you eat… just in case."

Clarisse understood the fear. People weren't supposed to see magic, and almost none ever did, with Charlie being the exception. However, it felt wise to avoid the risk. Choosing a dark restaurant, where Phil could occupy a table in relative seclusion, the couple went inside.

Ordering two meals, he winked at the waitress before she left them, but he could tell she had been disturbed by his doing so. "My girlfriend is invisible," he informed her in a teasing manner when she placed both plates before him. Sliding one over to the empty seat next to him, he cooed, "Aren't you, love?"

Immediately assuming the man needed psychiatric help, the woman grunted and turned away, calling over her shoulder, "Of course. We're happy you joined us this evening." Leaving him to his dinners, she didn't give the freak a second thought.

Folding his hands on the table before him, Phil glanced around at the high-backed, circular booth, which formed a pod around them. The opening only about three feet across, where patrons could slide into the cushioned seats, he observed, "This place is perfect. No one'll be able to see us except in passing as they walk by."

"Yes," Clarisse agreed. "I bet she even thinks you are eating my food for me," she giggled as she cut her steak and took a bite.

"So," he spoke just above a whisper, "How did you become a Forgotten Angel?"

"Charlie did it," she blurted, a warm flush spreading over her pale flesh. "I mean, I was a Summer Angel for over a hundred years. Then, when we were married, I became one of Karma's minions. I didn't really plan to; it just happened."

"Yeah," Phil sighed, "I don't think any of us ever intend to." Seeing the waitress passing by for the umpteenth time, he felt uncomfortable, as if she were spying on him. Noticing the dark curtain that hung next to him, he grasped it and flicked it across the narrow break in the seat, further cutting them off from prying eyes.

"That's better," she observed. "We'll have to remember this place and come back here often."

"Yeah," he relaxed into the seat, more comfortable with the covering to protect them.

"How did you become a part of Purgatory?" she probed more quietly. "If you don't mind my asking."

"I don't mind," he nodded, then ate a few bites of his meal. "I've never really talked about it before. Maybe it's time I shared."

Finishing her food while she listened, Clarisse felt a warm tingle wash over her. Charlie had been the love of her life, the half that made her whole, but something about the man next to her drew her in. She knew he was an empath, which is why he could sense her presence and hear her when she spoke to him. He had an awareness for others that went beyond the physical and the world of the living.

Pushing the thoughts aside, she focused on his warm voice as he described his life; the one he had lived before everything changed, and he became a Forgotten Angel.

TWENTY-THREE

In the Shadows

"I've only been one of Karma's minions for a few years," Phil began quietly. "I'm still in shock, really; at how it all happened." He pushed his plate back, leaving the remnants of his meal. "My wife and I were on vacation, driving across country. One minute, she was beside me, enjoying our day together, and the next, I was in a hospital bed, staring at the ceiling above me."

"You had an accident?" Clarisse instantly thought of Charlie.

"Yes," he shifted anxiously. "Apparently, another car crossed the double yellow line and hit us head on. Martha was killed instantly. They thought I would die, too, but I pulled through."

"Like Charlie," she sighed.

His body stiff, Phil ground his teeth. "I don't like Charlie, much, so please don't compare us."

"Why not? Has he done something to you?"

"No," Phil clipped, his eyes glazed for a moment. "He reminds me of my son."

"Oh," Clarisse breathed, not aware that Phil had any family to speak of.

"Yes," the man continued, "they're about the same age; well, Tony's a few years older. He's always been a good kid, but he made a few poor choices. That's how Karma got her hooks into me."

"Why? What did he do?" she inquired gently, seeing that telling his story caused him pain.

"Doesn't matter," Phil shook his head slightly. "Martha, my wife was a good woman. Fate took her from me, and drove my son nearly mad in the process. He got his life back on track, but Karma's keeping the score. If I get out of line, Tony's the one that will suffer."

Clarisse stared at his profile, considering his explanation. "You know about Fate?" she eventually demanded.

"Pfft," Phil spat. "I know a little. I pay attention and gather what I can. But I don't remember anything from the other side, if that's what you're asking."

"Charlie does," she confessed. "A great deal, in fact."

"Well, he's special," he sighed. "As much as I hate to say so, I've known since I first met him that he was trouble."

"When was this?" she prodded.

"I hitched a ride with them last year," he grinned deviously. "I was sent to talk to him about his mother. A real nice lady, Bethany is. Reminds me of Martha a bit."

"Karma sent you?" Clarisse asked in surprise.

"Nope. Someone else; someone I'd rather not mention," he cut his eyes over at the empty spot next to him. "But I'm sure she knew about it. Nothing gets past Karma."

"I've noticed," she sighed loudly. "So someone sent you to see him."

"Yes. And while we were talking, he mentioned being on a first name basis with Keeper."

"Oh my," she breathed, aware of the implication. "What do you really think is going on?"

"Plenty," a voice interrupted before Phil could reply. His eyes darting around anxiously, the man searched the booth he alone occupied.

"Gous!" Clarisse squealed, "What are you doing here?"

"Call it a friendly visit," the interloper hissed. "The two of you seem quite cozy. Where's your mate?"

"My mate is none of your business," she shrieked. "Phil and I are on a mission, and we have nothing to say to the likes of you."

"Easy, Clarisse," Phillip warned, having gathered that the male visitor occupied her world and not his.

"Yes," Gous implored, "relax and hear me out before you become excited."

Clarisse despised his turn of phrase. "You will never excite me," she bit back angrily. "But please, have your say and be gone."

A low laugh filled the small space. "My my, how easily riled," Gous gloated. "I've only come to share a bit of news. It seems that all is not well in the realm of Destiny and Fate, and a bit of a tiff seems to be brewing."

"What are you talking about, minion," she replied curtly, aware that he served the Darkness. "You do Fate's bidding. I'm sure that you would be pleased to find that he had taken the upper hand." She shuddered as the words fell from her lips, wondering how Keeper could allow such a thing.

"It's not Fate I speak of, for his followers are equally at risk," Gous replied in a gravely tone.

"Karma," Phil declared firmly. "She's up to something."

"Yes," Gous agreed, "but there in lies an opportunity. I have made an offer to a few of your kind; one that could usher in a new era on this planet. I'm here to include you in our plans."

"We have no plans," Clarisse informed him flatly. "You have dreams that will remain unfulfilled. Now, away with you before Karma overhears this and mistakes us as traitors."

Phil's eyes glistened, the idea of getting the better of their mistress more appealing than he could put into words. "Go on, Dark Angel," he whispered. "Don't upset our young friend here any further. Save your schemes for another day," he hinted.

"My schemes?" Gous replied, grinning at the pair across from him. "Then I shall count you in with us and will look for another time to share the details, where we will not be disturbed."

"Yes," Phil agreed, ready to leave the shadows of the private booth, "some other time."

TWENTY-FOUR

Only to Serve

CLARISSE TRANSPORTED Phil back to Purgatory three full days after they had departed. Each night they had dined at the same restaurant, drawing the curtain so she could eat in peace, safe from discovery. Every time, she had expected to be interrupted by their dark visitor, but he had not presented himself again.

No sooner had they arrived in the dining room, when Karma appeared. "So, Gous is after you," she asked Clarisse directly, as if she could see her.

"Gous has been after me for many years," the girl sighed, moving away from the shorter woman. Staring out of the glass next to the potted cacti, she sighed, "It's not anything new."

"But now you are part of my house," the group's leader cajoled. "You have nothing to say?" she addressed her companion instead.

"He's a sniveling punk," Phil informed her, turning to the kitchen in search of food. "He thinks he can recruit us; he wants to lead a rebellion against you, or the twins.... Or someone. I'm not even sure he knows who he wants to fight."

"Yes," Karma nodded, "and you have plans to join him?"

"I live only to serve the dispenser of justice," he replied without looking at her. He knew she could read his thoughts and his desire to be free of her was common knowledge. Locating a few steaks in the fridge, he pulled them out to fry.

"Why do you not ask me for a meal?" Karma suggested more quietly. "You know that I can provide you with whatever you desire."

"Because I don't want anything from you," Phil's angry tone escalated, taken by a wave of rage. "I eat your food, and my gut aches when I'm done!" he screamed.

Stepping back in surprise, Clarisse glanced between the two of them. In her private plane, she could observe their argument further, but chose to excuse herself. Turning to the stairs, she darted down them to search for Charlie, her long white gown flowing behind her as she moved.

Sensing that the girl had fled, Karma chuckled to herself. "Relax, Phil. We each know where we stand. I want you to help me with the Dark Angel."

"Help you," he sneered. "Help you how?" He didn't look at her and continued to prepare his lunch.

Shaking her head at his stubbornness, Karma sighed. "All right, make your own food, silly man." Turning to peer through the glass wall, she spoke in a low tone, "Gous is only one of many. A war is coming; one that will determine the course of this planet and the people that inhabit it. Be careful what side you choose; all who take the wrong side will be discarded." Turning to leave him, she strutted towards the stairs as well.

"Wait!" he called after her. "You didn't tell me what you want me to do with him."

"You must make your own choices," she paused her step, staring at the passage before her. "But if you serve me, gather what you can and share it with me; openly... freely. Do not make me scour your mind to sniff out the details of your treachery."

"Why do you keep me here?" he demanded, slamming a carton of milk on the counter and causing a small white geyser to briefly shoot out the top. "Why don't you destroy me and be done with it?"

A smile slowly curved her red lips, hidden from him as she faced the other way. "For all your complaining, this is your home. Nowhere else would you be free." Her heels dug into the plush carpet of the steps as she descended into the lower room with her fingers lightly trailing the banister. Before her, the cubicles expanded on either side of the set of aisles. On the far end, her office sat, the door closed and the blinds drawn over her window that overlooked the room.

To her right, a wall of glass separated the work area from the small gym. Inside, she could see Dante and Charlie lifting weights. She could not see the girl, but she knew she also occupied the smaller location. Shifting planes as she strutted through the entrance, she observed the girl hunched on a bench as she watched the two men and their flexing muscles.

"Clarisse," she called softly, causing the blonde to turn slightly. "Come with me, please."

Rising, the girl obeyed. Following her down the path to the other end of the great room, she sighed loudly. Inside the red-head's workspace, she closed the door and waited.

"How do you like working with Phil?" Karma asked without preamble, her voice crisp as she spoke.

"I'm fine with him," Clarisse lied, wishing she could spend her time with Charlie, instead.

"Indeed," Karma grimaced for an instant. "You still act as if your will is a private matter; I assure you that it is not."

Looking up at her, tears formed in Clarisse's crystal blue orbs. "Go on then," she sniffed. "What do you want from me?"

"I would like to see your seeker," Karma smiled. "Please, show me how it works."

Only hesitating for a moment, the blonde opened her hand and produced the device. Extending the appendage, she held the screen so they both could observe. "These were clients of mine," she explained in a soft voice.

"Yes," Karma exhaled loudly. "And?"

Touching her options one by one, she explained what each one did. The couple before them working on their yard, the man pushed a mower, while the woman appeared to be planting flowers along the front of the house. Clarisse recalled the night that Charlie had saved them from an attack by a burglar, who no doubt had been sent by Gous.

Sensing the girl's thoughts, Karma smiled. "You know things are different now," she stated quietly. She took the girl's hand and folded it so that the small white rectangle disappeared.

"Yes," Clarisse agreed. "I fear they will never be the same again."

"No, they will not," Karma soothed. "But your clients are safer, now that the Dark Angels have no reason to attack them; or should I say, no more reason than anyone else."

"I know," a tear escaped and trickled down to drip from her jaw. A sharp knock at the door interrupted them as Charlie pushed through the portal without waiting to be invited.

"Everything all right in here?" he asked quietly.

"Of course," Karma stepped away from his mate, hiding her irritation at his fondness for her. "Only a little girl-talk," she bounced around the desk and claimed her seat.

"I see," he slid his arm around Clarisse, lifting her chin so that her soft blue gaze met his. "Hello, angel."

"Hi, Charlie," she smiled back at him.

"You two should run along," Karma flicked the back of her hand at them, shewing them away as if they were children interrupting serious work. "Go have a day or two on your beach. I'll call if I need you."

Taking his love's hand, Charlie whisked them away in an instant, happy to have time alone with his wife.

TWENTY-FIVE

Young Love

"Isn't this fun!" Annalise called to Lorren as they strolled through a garden. Vines hung from the trees, while birds sang out around them.

"Sure," Lorren sounded less enthused. "It beats the middle of the desert, I guess."

"It sure does," Anna cupped a large magnolia flower, admiring the off-white petals and golden stems in the center. "So, how are you and Kari these days?"

Lorren paused, taken by surprise at the question. "We're fine, I guess." A teleporter with no telepathic abilities, it shocked her that Annalise would know about the couple and their blooming affair. Studying her for a long moment, she finally asked meekly, "Who told you?"

"Oh, young love is easy to see," Anna grinned mischievously. "I don't think there's a soul in Purgatory who doesn't know."

"Really?" Lorren gasped, the idea of their secret being known knocking the wind out of her. "Well, we haven't announced anything, so I really shouldn't say."

Annalise's laughter tinkled lightly in the fragrant air. "You don't need to announce. What you should do -"

"Thanks," the younger girl interrupted her, facing her squarely, "But I'm sure I have this covered. I think we need to get back to our targets."

Shaking her head, Anna felt sad that the girl had cut their conversation short. She had little opportunity for sharing, since Portia had vacated their room. Clarisse still occupied the space, but she being in the other plane had complicated their relationship. Charlie had suggested a setup using a baking tray and a bottle of baby powder, and that had at least allowed the roommates to share a few conversations, but it wasn't the same as speaking to a live person.

"Ok," she sighed reluctantly, dropping her flower and preparing to transport them as soon as Lorren communicated the destination.

An instant later, a pair of men bolted through the shrubs. Catching her by surprised, one of them knocked Anna to the ground and rendered her unconscious while landing blow after blow to her small frame.

Her eyes wide with fright, Lorren made an attempt to enter the men's thoughts. She wanted to coerce them into giving up the attack, but found their minds guarded, protected by some kind of barrier. A sharp jab landing against her cheek, she fell to the ground and covered her head. Sobbing loudly, she cried out, mentally screaming for help.

Charlie, Dante, and Kari all heard her cry. Instantly transporting to her location, Charlie and Dante wasted no time bringing a few of the vines to life and using them to subdue the two attackers, at least long enough to transport everyone to Purgatory.

Dropping each of the girls on one of the couches in the atrium, Dante stormed around the room, pacing like a lion defending his pride. Glancing around anxiously, as if someone could have followed them, he growled, "Everyone ok?"

"No," Kari clipped in panic. "Lorren's been hurt!"

Charlie dropped to his knees next to the girl, observing that her face was badly cut, and that she had been beaten severely before they had arrived. Taking her hand in his, he mingled their spirits to calm her. "*It's ok, Lorren. I'm here,*" he comforted her telepathically.

Assessing their other housemate, Dante informed them, "Anna isn't any better; I think she's going into shock."

"She's pale, raise the tail," Kari stated anxiously, snatching a few cushions from the back of the sofa and placing them under her feet.

"What?" Charlie demanded, confused by the brief phrase.

"It's a trick for remembering how to treat a shock victim," Dante soothed, recalling having heard it before. "*Pale raise the tail, red, raise the head.* You look at their face and decide which course is best."

"Oh," Charlie agreed with a small nod, turning Lorren's hand over to Kari. "Here, you hold her. I'm goin' back t' deal with those two goons."

"No, you're not," Dante wrapped his firm grasp around the younger man's arm. "We got the girls away; we stay put and inform Karma before we do anything else."

Yanking himself free, Charlie could feel the rage creeping up his neck and flushing his face. "I am a dispenser of justice, an' those two deserve t' be punished!"

"Save it for later, mate," Kari warned. "Karma won't forget their debt. Besides, it seems a little odd they would attack any of us, don't you think?"

Glaring at the blond with his chest heaving, Charlie's mind remained clouded by adrenaline. Blinking a few times, he could hear the words, but their meaning became lost in the shroud of anger that engulfed him.

"Charlie!" he heard Clarisse's voice cutting through the haze.

"What?" he coughed, looking around and realizing by the number of people in the room that he had blacked out for a moment or two. "Where did everyone come from so fast?"

"Fast? You've been in a trance for about five minutes," Dante bit sharply, coming down hard on his underling. "You need to get a serious grip on that temper of yours, buddy. Someday, it's going to cost you."

It already has, Charlie silently admitted to himself. Crossing the plane, he located Clarisse and pulled her into his arms. "It's ok; I'm ok," he rubbed her arm firmly as she shed actual tears. "Baby, what's the matter?" He didn't think she felt that strongly about either of the girls, so her reaction mystified him.

"They were attacked," she spoke between ragged breaths. "Like my clients used to be."

"Yeah," he agreed, squeezing her tighter, "I bet it was Gous."

"Maybe," Karma joined them, ushering them into the great room on the other side of the house. "But we can't be sure without a bit of investigation."

Following her lead, the pair moved to one of the sets of chairs that formed the two large conversation areas and sat down. Stroking her hand, arm, and back, in turns, Charlie continued to comfort his wife. "It's ok, love. They'll be ok; you can't blame yourself for this."

A tray of tea appeared on the table before them. Taking one of the small cups and pouring in a bit of the golden liquid, Charlie glanced at the woman who had taken a seat on the couch across from them. "Thanks," he offered. "This'll calm her a bit."

"Yes," Karma agreed, waiting for the pair to be ready for instruction.

Catching the silky cascade that hung between them, Charlie pushed her hair back and lifted her chin. "Here, baby; take a sip." Helping her to hold the fine china steady, the edge touched her lips and she noisily drew a swallow from the top.

"That's good," she breathed quietly. "Always tasty when Karma makes it." She smiled weakly in an attempt to appear more at ease.

"Just relax," Karma implored, her back stiff as she sat, hands in her lap. Her typical red suit a nice contrast to her dark skin, she appeared genuinely concerned over the incident.

A few minutes and a second cup later, Clarisse appeared to have regained control of her faculties. "I'm ok," she said more firmly.

"Good," Karma rose, pacing slightly as she dismissed the service tray and its contents. "I have a small task for the two of you. It must be you, since you know who it is that I need."

"Who you need?" Charlie stood, an uneasy feeling twisting his gut. "What're you talkin' about?"

"I need to speak to Father," she informed him directly.

"Father!" Clarisse gasped, also finding her feet. Recalling that she had already stated she knew all of the light angels, as well as the dark ones, it shocked her more that she would actually send them after him.

"Surly you are joking," Charlie shook his head. "That old codger is a waste o' time. He speaks in riddles an' never tells you anything you wanna know."

"Well, perhaps I can be a bit more persuasive," Karma smiled at his assessment. "Either way, I must speak to him at once."

"Ok," Charlie agreed reluctantly. "How do we find him?"

Karma cut her eyes over at the girl, waiting for her to reply. Glaring back at her for a long moment, Clarisse finally opened her hand and said quietly, "I can do it."

Staring at the device that lay in her palm, Charlie gasped, "Where did you get that?"

"I've had it ever since Destiny gave it back to me; after I came back from being Donna. I thought she would take it away from me, but she hasn't. I've been scared to use it, though," she confessed quietly.

Steadying her hand, Charlie thought about the dream, the one that was actually a memory of the time she had shown him how to use a seeker before. "Wow," he breathed, aware that Karma had left them. "Well, I guess we go bag us an ol' man and drag his ass back here, asap. See if Karma can make him tell us what's really goin' on."

TWENTY-SIX

Old Enemies

THE MINUTES TICKED by while Clarisse accessed client after client. "I don't think that he will be associated with any of my charges," she confessed.

"Can you peek in on any o' his?" Charlie whispered, feeling odd about the deceptiveness of their actions.

"Yes, I did that last time," she recalled the previous time they had needed to find the oldest of the Light Angels. "But I don't have access to all of them; only a few. Give me a minute, and let me try a few other tricks."

Watching the flicker of the screen, Charlie frowned. "Well, shit."

"What's the matter?" she glanced up at his twisted features.

"Is that where he is?" he indicated the image.

"That's that girl, isn't it," Clarisse watched the plump figure behind a register making change for someone.

"Yeah, the one you ruined my date with," he accused before playfully kissing her cheek. "It's ok, love. We have each other now, so le's not fight over th' past."

The scene still playing out before them, Brett came into view and slapped Tabs on the bottom. "Son of a bitch," Charlie growled as he watched his arch rival bend over and kiss his former best friend.

Her brow furrowed, Clarisse did not feel any better seeing the two of them together. "She is one of Father's charges," she confessed softly. "Perhaps we can locate him there."

"You bet we can," Charlie grasped her arm firmly and transported them to the Dairy Queen. Moving within the safety of the magical plane, he walked among his old enemies with ease. "You'd think these guys would grow up and get some real jobs," he announced as he watched Brett and Tabitha working side by side.

"I think he's the manager here," Clarisse informed him, still studying her device. "You've been gone a year, and much has changed in your absence."

"Yeah," he agreed, still glowering at the couple. "I haven't been back since we sold the house. As a matter of fact, Brett's daddy bought it." Unable to restrain himself any longer, he delved into Tabitha's mind, unable to believe the joy that emanated from her as she carried on with the boy that had made their lives hell.

"Oh my God," he gasped.

"What is it?" Clarisse closed her hand, darkening the device for the time being. "I'll try again in a few minutes."

"She's pregnant," his voice shook, his hands forming fists at his side. "The sorry bastard got her knocked up!"

Catching his arm before he pounced on the unsuspecting male, Clarisse pointed out in a gentle rebuke, "I think they're married, hun. Look at her fingers." Sure enough, the gold band caught the light as she moved to wipe down tables.

His mouth hanging open, Charlie stared as she worked, her belly hiding her unborn child. *I can't believe she married him.* "Why would she do such a thing?" he asked hoarsely.

"Because they fell in love," Father announced in his booming round voice.

"Father!" Clarisse exclaimed, overtaken with joy to see her old mentor. "I did what you asked," she informed him after she had hugged him firmly. Standing up straight, she showed him her ring. "We're married now as well."

"Yes," the old man smiled, "and rightly so."

Turning to the pair, Charlie growled, "We need to take this somewhere else. I'm gonna be sick if I stay here any longer." Pushing them towards the door, he led them out to the sidewalk and down the path that ran next to the road. Once they were a safe distance from the store, he stopped to face Father squarely. "Karma wants to see you," he stated flatly.

"Yes, I am aware," Father agreed. "However, I will pay her a visit in my own time."

"I don' think it works that way," Charlie towered over him. "Too much crazy shit goin' on, an' I'm in no mood to argue. We're going back t' Purgatory, an' you're goin' with us."

"Am I?" Father ambled along the trail, making his way closer to Charlie's childhood home. Arriving at the driveway, he paused to stare up at the stately old structure. A ladder lay leaned against the side and men moved about, making repairs and adding a new coat of paint to the outside.

"They're fixin' it up," Charlie observed, a tremor in his voice. The town had never had more than a couple of thousand residents, and he wondered who would be fool enough to move to such a limited environment. "Maybe Brett's dad is gonna re-sell it," he observed hopefully.

"Tabitha and Brett own it now," Father folded his hands over his large round belly. "From what I can tell, your room is going to be the nursery."

"Stop it," Clarisse bit angrily. "Why are you torturing him so? Can't you see it hurts him, to know that the two of them ended up together?"

"My dear Clarisse, why should Charlie be bothered by it? She was nothing more than a play thing to him. He never had any intention of taking care of her; of making a life with her. She was convenient, nothing more," Father rubbed salt in Charlie's fresh wounds.

"How would you know what she meant to me? It's not like -" Charlie stopped abruptly, the inkling of a memory catching light and shining brightly. "You knew who I was," he accused. "When Clarisse was training me, after I died. We met you, and you said you knew who I was."

"Of course I knew," Father chuckled. "You and Tabitha were inseparable as children, all the way through high school. It would have been impossible for me to be her guardian and not at least be aware of your existence."

Charlie stared at him, his chest heaving. Something about the old man hadn't felt right, even from the beginning. His practiced lies held deception, Charlie felt sure of it.

"Be careful, Charlie," the elder man warned, "I see rage in your eyes. Be sure it does not consume you."

"Shut up," the boy bit angrily. "We've listened t' you for too long, taken you at your word too many times. Karma wants t' see you. We go to Purgatory, now, or you an' I are gonna find out which one o' us is the strongest."

"Charlie!" Clarisse gasped, unable to believe her ears. "How dare you threaten Father! Have you any idea who he is?"

"No, I don' have a clue," he didn't take his eyes off his target, "An' neither do you. What I do know is that secrets and lies have surrounded this guy for longer than you've been around, an' he's sucked us into them. Him an' his alien friends."

"Oh, Charlie; don't be so dramatic," Father chuckled, stepping towards him and extending a hand.

Refusing to take the appendage, Charlie slapped it away, "You heard me, old man. Purgatory. Now. And don' make me say it again."

TWENTY-SEVEN

Imperfect Being

THE AIR of the house felt cool around them when the trio landed in the atrium. Looking down at the couches, Charlie could see the stains of blood on the furniture where his friends had lain only a few hours before. The house seemed calm, and for a moment he felt panic that they had taken too long in their mission. Reaching out mentally to Karma, he demanded, *"Where are the girls?"*

"They're resting in their rooms," she supplied in kind before appearing next to him, smiling that he had chosen to contact her in the intimate manner. "Father," she said aloud, offering him her hand.

Taking her fingers, the older man raised them to his lips, kissing them lightly. "My dear Karma. Always a pleasure."

Clarisse took Charlie's hand, her digits trembling. Life had been so simple only a short time ago. A Summer Angel, she had been content to flit about the world, helping people to have better lives. Now one of Karma's minions, she felt lost and alone, even with her husband by her side.

"He's delivered," Charlie stated loudly, giving the girl a squeeze. "I don' think you need us for the rest…"

"No," Karma agreed, dismissing them, "I'll take it from here."

Transporting them to their beach, Charlie dropped into the soft earth, his knees buckling beneath him. Burying his face in his hands, a strong gust of wind blew against him, carrying the smell of salt water and sanctuary on the air.

Hearing him sob, Clarisse ran her hands over his broad shoulders. "Don't cry, love," she pleaded.

"I can't help it," he sniveled, pulling her down in front of him and then into his arms. Hugging her tightly, as if she were the only strip of reality that remained, he gasped. "It's wrong. Everything's wrong. Nothing in my life has ever been what it seemed."

Unable to deny his claims, she held him, her own tears falling unchecked. "I'm so sorry, love. If I had known, I swear to you I would have said. I never would have kept the truth from you."

"I know," he relaxed his hold, allowing her to sink into the granules so he could stare into her eyes. Tracing the line of her jaw, he clenched his teeth, baring them in anger. "They lied t' you, too. Used you, maybe even worse than they used me."

Her lip trembling, she nodded her agreement. "What will we do?"

"I don' know. I feel like you're Donna, an' I'm about t' lose you all over again."

"No," she panted, shaking her head slowly, "Not this time." Getting to her feet, she offered him her hand.

Placing his digits into her warm palm, he stood, admiring how her eyes fell only an inch or so below his. "I'm sorry," he stammered.

"Don't be sorry," she breathed, placing her lips against his stubbled cheek. "I love you as you are; an imperfect being in an imperfect world." Her fingers dug into his flesh, moving up his chest and forcing the thin material of his shirt upwards with them.

In the blink of an eye, Charlie removed the garment for her, allowing her to feel the hardness of his muscles unimpeded. The fire kindled within him, he sighed. "How can you think o' makin' love at a time like this?"

"How can you not?" she challenged, pushing him towards the bed he had made for her.

"Temptress," he breathed, catching her mouth and crushing her lips beneath his. Moaning, he discarded her clothing with no more than a thought, and traced the line of her bare ribs with his fingers. Hoisting her into his arms, he stepped onto the platform. The fine material of the walls caught in the wind and rustled around them.

Lowering her onto the mattress, he sighed, "I will never get enough of you." Hovering over her, he paused, his fingers sliding over her smooth skin.

"Charlie," she whimpered, fire burning within her. Only one man had ever touched her; as Donna, she had broken off her relationship with her body's previous boyfriend without ever knowing him in the flesh. As Clarisse, there had only ever been one. Lifting her face, she kissed him, then sucked on his lip. Her fingers buried in his brown curls, the tips tingled against his scalp.

Feeling him against her, he panted, and her breaths grew light and quick. "I will consume you," he whispered against her ear, sending shivers to the depths of her being.

"Yes," she hissed, lost in their throws of passion. Clarisse didn't care anymore about Karma or Keeper. The twins didn't matter, and Father meant nothing to her. She had found her place; in the arms that she would give anything for, and the love she would do anything to protect.

TWENTY-EIGHT

Karma's Desire

PURGATORY APPEARED in total darkness when Charlie and Clarisse arrived home the following night. They had spent two days in their love nest, enjoying the pleasures of one another's flesh, only pausing long enough to eat when they could no longer resist. Eventually falling into exhausted slumber, the pair had awoken at sunset and decided they had stayed away as long as they dared.

Standing in the atrium, Charlie clasped Clarisse's fingers firmly and guided her through the house. The kitchen empty, they passed through the narrow hall and into the great room on the other side. Finding the sitting areas equally deserted, the pair climbed the stairs, suspecting their housemates might be asleep.

Peeking into the first two rooms, all of the beds were empty and the chairs unoccupied. The bathrooms and showers sat in silence, also unused at the moment. In their rooms on the far end, Charlie could see that Kari did not lie in his bunk, nor did Annalise in hers. "Where the hell is everyone?" he growled, drawing Clarisse closer to him in a protective manner.

Descending the stairs on their end, they arrived in the kitchen. Making the turn onto the next set of steps, they quickly surveyed the offices in the basement, finding them to also be deserted.

Climbing to the first floor, a flash of lightning lit up the space, bright through the glass walls; a moment later, thunder rumbled nearby. "Wow, that was close," he breathed, still holding her close to him. "I wonder where everyone has gone?"

A torrent of rain slammed against the house, a loud roar filling the space. "This doesn't feel right," he guided her over to the window where they could watch the deluge. "It's hasn't rained a single time since I've been here."

"What do you think is causing it?" she whispered back.

Seeing the barn through the darkness, illuminated by flashes of light, he replied, "I'm not sure. But there's one more place we can look."

"I've never been in there," Clarisse informed him.

"No, I don' suppose that you have," he agreed; "Tha's Karma's private space. But, it's the only place left, an' I think we should take a peek." Grasping her fingers firmly, he transported them into Karma's haven.

A clap of thunder echoed as soon as they materialized in the center of the dimly lit room. All around the walls, small fires danced at the tops of slender candles. The dark, heavy curtains hung in place, hiding the screens that Karma used for viewing the world outside.

His eyes ready after the darkness of the house, Charlie gasped at the circle of Forgotten Angels, all on their knees and facing Karma in their center. "Good of you to join us," she said when he noticed her.

Leaving Clarisse alone in the magical plane, he became visible to the others. "Uh, hi," he stammered. "Mind if we ask what's going on?"

"Not at all," Karma raised her arm, the sleeve of her long red gown hanging from the appendage in a shimmering cascade that almost reached the floor. "We've been sharing what we know about those who stand against us."

"Oh," Charlie shuddered at the raspy sound of her voice. "Well, would you like for us to stay?"

"Absolutely," Karma agreed, motioning for two of their comrades to make room for them. Inching their way around, the gaps between the rest grew more narrow as sufficient space was created between Portia and Dante.

Taking a knee next to his friend, Charlie could feel Clarisse's presence as she slid in between him and the other female. Clearing his throat anxiously, he addressed Karma in the calmest voice he could muster; "What would you have of us?"

"Open your minds to me," she implored, moving to stand before him. She had promised him at their joining that his thoughts would be his own, but for the moment, she needed to be clear in his intentions.

Dropping his head back, Charlie stared at the shadows playing on the ceiling above them. Relaxing into the chaotic rhythm, he exhaled loudly, willing himself to share with her. A tingle ran through his body, as if she were holding him as she had some months ago when he had pledged himself to her.

Clarisse whimpered softly beside him, but he remained completely focused on their leader. He inhaled deeply and pushed the air out through his nose, causing his nostrils to flare. Closing his brown orbs, the seconds ticked by until Karma spoke, her tone sounding more normal; "You are all free to go."

Confused, Charlie opened his eyes to look around. Seeing everyone accounted for, except the visitor he had delivered a few days before, he asked, "What was this about, exactly?"

"Time is moving faster," Karma smiled. "Quickly it runs through the hourglass, carrying us towards the choices that must be made; to the fight that must be won at all cost."

"Fight," he parroted, getting to his feet, "what fight, Karma? I'm gettin' tired of your games," he clipped, wondering if the examination had anything to do with Father's visit.

"Don't worry," she soothed, her hand indicated the house through the wall, "The hour is close, but has not arrived."

Not convinced, he repeated, "Who's gonna fight against us? You know that me an' Clarisse will stand up for you; we've taken your side."

"I know that you have; I have seen it in your eyes and felt it in your mind only a moment ago," she insisted. "Go inside, out of the storm. I have searched all the souls in Purgatory, and found all to be worthy of my house."

Charlie heard her words and cut his gaze over to glare at Phillip.

"What about him?" he indicated the older man doubtfully.

"I have a special path for him to walk," Karma smiled mysteriously. "Do not trouble your heart over him. He will serve his purpose soon enough."

Thinking they were going to get rid of him, Charlie grinned to himself, a twist of pleasure in his gut at the idea of finally seeing the other man removed. Squaring his shoulders, he waited as the others disappeared, presumably to turn in for the night. "I'll see you in a few minutes," he informed Clarisse, sending her away with them, but unable to see the displeasure etched on her face.

"Karma, I hate t' disagree with you in front o' the others," he began, but she shot him a look that stopped him cold.

"Then don't," she retorted sharply. "I guard my secrets closely, and you have heard all that is meant for your ears."

His jaw rocking from side to side, he waited. When he showed no sign of obeying, she scolded, "You are a stubborn man, Charles Phillips."

"Yeah," he nodded anxiously; "Give me somethin'," he implored. "Anything that'll make me feel better about all o' this."

Exhaling loudly, Karma glared at him. "Phil will do his part, as will you. I have another reward for you, for your service, but I'm not ready to divulge it yet. Now be gone, before you force me to punish you," her eyes darted up and down his tall frame. "Or do you desire my company for the evening?" she teased in a gravelly voice, her desire unmistakable.

"Punish me," he chuckled, recalling that things had gone relatively smoothly inside Purgatory since Clarisse had agreed to join them. "I doubt that you would; an' no, I don' need your *company*, so I'll leave." Materializing in his room, he could instantly feel Clarisse's presence and shifted to her plane.

"I thought you were going to bed," he stated stiffly.

"I was waiting to say goodnight," she raised her chin defiantly.

Charlie glared at her for a moment before taking her in his arms, aware that she had wanted to be sure that he slept in his own bed. Hugging her firmly, he sighed, "Sorry, love. Go get some sleep. We shouldn't waste time or energy on worry. I'm sure this's all gonna work out eventually."

TWENTY-NINE

Visiting Hours

CHARLIE SMOOTHED the front of his suit with one hand, a large bouquet of flowers gripped in the other. Staring at the numbered panel, the floor to his mother's office glowed dimly. *Just breathe,* he reminded himself. He had spoken to her each week as promised, but he had not been for an actual visit since going to Purgatory, almost five months prior. *Too long.*

Karma had arranged their evening together; a surprise for both of them, she said. Charlie had been nervous ever since she informed him of the event, and tried desperately to remain calm. Keeping his secret when all he could do was make objects move had been hard enough; *how am I going to hide all that I am now?*

Stepping off the elevator, he exhaled loudly and then turned to the left. Following the hallway, he arrived outside of the marketing firm where she worked. Seeing the glass doors, he paused. *What the hell?*

BETHANY PHILLIPS appeared in gold block letters; the bottom of six names, but it was there. *Did she get a promotion?* Pushing on the entrance, Charlie squared his shoulders and prepared himself to find out. "I'm here to see Beth Phillips," he advised the young woman behind the front desk.

"One moment," the girl replied, lifting the phone and pressing a button. "Ms. Phillips? There's a young man here to see you."

Charlie shifted his weight from one foot to the other; he could hear her muffled voice through the device. Unable to make out his mother's words, all he could do was wait.

"Oh, he's young… handsome. Brown wavy hair and heavenly brown eyes," the girl grinned as she described him. "And he's in a suit."

On the other end of the line, Beth considered who could be there when her calendar was empty. Eventually giving in, she stated. "I'll come and get him." Hanging up, she shuffled a few things on her desk so she could find her place when she returned, then stood and strutted down the hall. Turning the corner, her jaw dropped in surprise, "Charlie!"

Grinning sheepishly, he shifted the flowers from one hand to the other; "Hello, mom."

Her navy business dress fit her frame perfectly, accentuating the curves he had never known she had. Stepping towards him, she squeezed him tightly and tears streamed down her face. Wiping at them quickly, she ushered him down the hall, stammering, "My office is this way, son."

Glancing into the offices that they passed, he observed men and women at tables and desks, all working diligently on various projects. When he arrived at his mother's, he stepped inside, his mouth briefly opening in awe. Before him stood a large table at the perfect height to work at while standing, but two chairs sat next to it for sitting as well. Along the far left wall, a large desk stood, and a floor to ceiling window made up the exterior behind it.

"Holy shit, mom," he shoved his offering at her. "This isn't the job you got!" Arriving at the window, he stared down at the street below, "Is it?"

"Well, yes and no," she beamed, sniffing at a few of the buds before pushing a button on her phone and announcing, "Alice, do we have a vase around here we can put these in?"

"Yes, ma'am," the receptionist replied. "I'll bring one in."

Clicking again to end the connection, Beth bit her bottom lip for a moment. Looking down at herself, she flushed, "I guess you're not the only one who's been rehabilitating."

"No kidding," he replied, his voice taking on a hint of anger. "How much weight have you lost?" he indicated the lighter Beth standing before him.

"About fifty pounds," she smiled up at him. "And this is the same company, but I was promoted after about six weeks."

"Yeah, your name is on the door!" he clipped, indicating towards the entrance with a flat palm.

"Well, all of our names are on the door," she smiled brightly. "They like what I can do. And I've been practicing, you know; letting go of my negativity. It's been hard some days," she sighed loudly, "But I'm really getting better at it."

At that moment, the young woman from the front joined them, offering a vase made of clear glass. Seeing the water inside of it, Charlie helped her set it on the table smoothly. "Thanks," she grinned politely before leaving them to their discussion.

Hesitating, Charlie wished he could start over. He didn't want his mother to think he was upset; on the contrary, he was more proud of her at that moment than he had ever been in his life. "I'm here to take you to dinner," he offered quietly. "I haven't made it for visitation in months, so I don't have to worry about going back tonight; tomorrow is fine."

"I'd like that," Beth continued to grin as she arranged her gift into the vase. "Let me take care of a few things here, and we'll go. Do you have somewhere in particular in mind?"

"We have reservations at The Bazaar," he supplied more calmly. "Get what you need; we have about two hours to get there."

"All right," she moved to her desk and began clearing things away. Putting her current project into a large folder, she spoke softly. "I'm sorry I didn't tell you about the promotion. Or the diet."

"It's ok," he mumbled, inspecting the items on her large shelving unit that ran along the wall straight in front of the office entrance. At the far end, he noticed a door. Taking the handle firmly, he pulled it open to reveal a private bathroom. Pretending he had known that was what lay behind it, he excused himself, closing the large wooden cover behind him when he was safely inside; *shit*.

Relieving himself, he turned to the granite-topped vanity. Leaning on it with stiff elbows, he inspected himself in the mirror. He had shaved for the occasion, removing the thin layer of stubble he typically wore these days, and the eyes staring back at him seemed hollow. *What the hell is wrong with you?* he demanded of the image. *She's doing great; don't be an ass about it!*

Splashing cool water on his face, he used one of the soft towels hanging on the rack to pat his skin dry. Smiling at his reflection, he coached himself to hold the gesture and be happy for the woman who had raised him. Exiting the cubical, he apologized, "I'm sorry I reacted so strongly. You surprised me," he chuckled. "I'm happy for you, mom."

Her desk in order, Bethany stood at the tall table, admiring the bouquet. "It's quite all right, baby," she replied. "I understand. We've both changed; for the better from the looks of it," she indicated her son with an open palm.

Charlie stiffened, noticing for the first time that his mother's accent had all but vanished. "Have you been taking speech lessons, or something?" he tried not to sound accusatory.

"I have," she flushed, "I've been learning to sound more... professional. It helps with communicating with clients."

"So, on the phone..." his voice trailed away.

"Oh, it comes back when I'm not thinking about it," she flushed, "Especially when I'm talking to someone who has a bit o' southern drawl," she lapsed for a moment.

"Nice," he nodded. Feeling awkward, he indicated the door. "Well, shall we?"

"Yes," she agreed, picking up her purse and hanging it over her shoulder. Following him to the elevator, they climbed off on the first floor, where a large black car awaited them. "Thank you, Henry," she addressed the valet before sliding into the driver's seat.

Taking the passenger side, Charlie looked around the leather interior anxiously, "Mom, where's my car?" he demanded loudly.

"Your car is fine, baby. It's parked at the apartment. This one's mine," she grinned, suddenly overcome with pride.

Looking over the dash of the new BMW, Charlie could feel a lump in his gut he doubted had anything to do with hunger. Not only had his mother been successful in his absence, she had thrived. He had felt guilty at the idea of lying to her, and had even worried about what would become of her if he did not return to their apartment and their lives together. He could see now that she didn't need him; she could handle things just fine on her own.

THIRTY

Party Crasher

LOOKING around as they made their way to their table, Charlie could feel his heart in his throat; *damn, this place is nice.* Fortunately for him, Karma was picking up the tab; otherwise they might have ended up in the back washing dishes after the meal. Taking a seat in a single chair on his side, his mother faced him on a long couch. "This is pretty unusual," he commented aloud.

"Yes," his mother agreed. "I've been here a few times with clients. The food is delicious and the décor really adds to the experience."

Picturing the Dairy Queen that had constituted eating out when he was growing up, he felt shocked by how much things had changed. Shaking his head, Charlie stared at his lap to hide his grin. "I can't believe you sound so different."

Her laughter low, she flushed with pride. "I've been working very hard on myself. I only wish your father could see me now," she sighed, opening her menu. "I'll take the sautéed shrimp," she informed the waiter who arrived a moment later.

Glancing down the list, Charlie nodded, "I'll have the same."

As soon as they were alone, Beth asked, "Do you think your father can see me now?"

Choking on his sip of wine, her son faltered, "What do you mean by that?"

"Well, you know," she toyed with her napkin, "Do you think he's in heaven, looking down on us? I think he would be so proud of us; both of us! Sitting here together, enjoying a meal without any bickering," she beamed. "I hope that he is."

"Yeah, me too," he raised his glass to her before gulping several large swallows. Changing the subject, he worked his way through the list of questions he had prepared before making his way to L.A. He hoped to keep things on an even keel and avoid topics that might lead to uncomfortable conversations. Starting with Aunt Belinda, he mentioned people they both knew who could be used for suitable topics. Soon, their meal arrived, and the need to keep up his end of the discussion lessened.

"Oh my God, this is delicious!" he exclaimed after a few bites.

"Yes, this is my favorite dish," she informed him. A few minutes later, she indicated her glass, "I need a refill."

Spying their waiter, Charlie telepathically nudged him to return to their table, then said, "Here he comes," aloud.

"Here who comes?" Phil asked, taking the empty seat on the sofa next to Beth.

Charlie's mouth fell open in shock, "What are you doing here?" he demanded, snapping his teeth shut and grinding them together.

"I'm having dinner, or was," the man across from him grinned deviously. "I noticed the two of you and just had to stop by and see how you were doing."

"Phil, is that you?" Bethany breathed, a warm flush coloring her cheeks.

"Ah, you do remember me," he smiled at her. "I wondered if I had over-stepped my bounds."

"For the second time, yes!" Charlie snapped. "We didn' invite you t' sit with us last time, an' we sure as hell don' want you here now!"

"Charlie, please!" Beth intervened, glancing around anxiously, "Don't be rude." She turned to the older man and asked, "How have you been?" as if they were old friends.

At that moment, the waiter arrived to refill her drink. "Would the gentleman like a glass as well?" he asked, holding up an empty.

"Yes, please," Phil nodded approvingly. Accepting his libation, he turned to her; "I've been well," he answered Beth's question without missing a beat. "I'm here on business and recognized you; I couldn't bear the thought of leaving without saying hello," his voice dripped with honey as his fingers toyed with the fresh glass of wine on the table before him.

"I'm so glad you did!" she placed her hand on his. "I'm so sorry you had to leave before I could say goodbye last time. I enjoyed your company very much."

Charlie watched as Phil curled her fingers into his. *"What the hell are you doing?"* he demanded telepathically, forcing a smile onto his lips at the same time.

"Oh, now you're ready to share a little covert conversation," Phil countered.

"This isn't the same as you randomly reading my thoughts," Charlie insisted. *"Why don't you get the hell out of here and let me enjoy the evening with my mother?"*

"I think I'd like a bit of desert," Bethany stated as she finished the last bite of her meal. "Tonight is a special occasion, after all."

"It sure is," Phil agreed, "Would you like to split something chocolate with me?"

Charlie could no longer hold the fake expression, and a deep scowl crinkled his features. "Mom," he stated flatly, "I really think *Phil* should be on his way. I don't get to see you that often..." his voice trailed away, seeing that she hardly noticed his presence.

"Relax, Charlie," the party crasher said aloud, then tacked on mentally, *"Didn't I warn you about poisoning her life?"*

"I'm not," he tossed back bitterly. *"We're having dinner, for Christ's sake."*

"Yes, but I could tell that you were struggling. Let me help you. I can steer the conversation to things that she'll enjoy talking about; things that will be safe to discuss at the same time. Call it a favor."

"Some favor," Charlie mumbled, snatching up his glass and leaning back in his chair dejectedly.

"What favor?" Bethany asked, still toying with Phil's hand.

"Oh, nothing," her son lied flatly, "I was just thinking about owing someone when I get back to the center."

"Oh," her features darkened for a moment, as if she had forgotten why he had been away. "I'm sorry, baby. I shouldn't be wasting our evening," she glanced at him, then back at Phil.

"That's quite all right," the man next to her patted her hand, "But if you'll agree to have dinner with me tomorrow night, I'd be more than happy to wait my turn." His grin covering his face from ear to ear, he awaited her reply.

Opening her handbag, she retrieved a business card. "This has my office and my cell," she informed him. "How long will you be in town?"

"For a few days," he assured her, running his thumb lightly across the embossed lettering. "Thanks, Beth. I'll give you a call tomorrow and we can arrange for a real date." Standing, he left the two of them as quickly as he had arrived.

Charlie cringed; *real date, my ass!* His blood boiling, he couldn't wait to get back to Purgatory; *see what Karma has to say about this!*

The remainder of their meal strained, Beth and Charlie returned to their small apartment as soon as they had finished. Putting on a pair of shorts and a tee-shirt to sleep in, he met her in the living area for a bit more discussion before they went to sleep. Noticing that she wore a broad smile, he commented aloud, hoping to smooth things over between them, "I'm glad you're so happy I made it for a visit."

"Oh," Beth curled her feet beneath her on their sofa, "I'm sorry, hun. I was just thinking about running into Phil again. It almost seems like fate that we were meant to know each other. Or would that be destiny?"

"Neither," Charlie flopped back in the over-stuffed chair and crossed his arms. Breathing out an angry huff of air, he snapped, "Look, mom; about Phil. I thought he was a fruitcake las' time we met. The fact that he jus' walks up to total strangers an' sits at their tables has got t' say somethin' about his character."

"Well, sure it does!" the woman across from him agreed brightly. "It says that he's an open and friendly person. Do you think he finds me attractive?"

The color drained from Charlie's features. "Mom!" he glowered at her, "what about dad?"

"Baby, your father's been gone over a year," she frowned. "Or have you forgotten?"

Glaring at her, he realized it was too soon to get into that conversation. *I'm sure Karma will handle Phil as soon as I tell her what's going on,* he assured himself. "No, mom; I haven't forgotten," he said aloud.

"Then you have to understand," her lips drew into thin lines, her brow taking a pair of deep creases. "I've been on several dates, since you've been away."

The air trapped in his lungs, Charlie's face went from ghost white to bright red. "You've been dating?" he asked more forcefully.

"Yes, baby. I'm a fairly young woman, you know. Forty-two is barely middle aged, an' you can't expect me t' spend the rest o' my life alone!" her accent grew thicker, a sure sign she had become upset.

"Calm down, mom. I'm not asking you t' be alone. I jus' think that Phillip Parson isn't the right type o' man for you, tha's all," he offered more calmly.

"After one conversation with him, you think you can tell? I happened t' like him, an' I'm gonna date him if I want to," she leapt to her feet. "In fact, I think I'll go to bed now. I'll be up at six, an' I can drive you to the airport." Turning her back on him, she stomped to her room and closed the door angrily before he could reply.

Staring after her for a while, he thought about going in and telling her how sorry he was. The last thing he wanted to do was upset her. In the end, he decided to leave well enough alone. Besides, he had his car, there wasn't any need to wait for her to wake up. *Airport?* She thought he had flown into town. *Well, I never have told her where Purgatory's located.* And furthermore, he wasn't going to.

Going into his room, Charlie slipped off the sleep-clothes and put on plain old jeans and a tee from the few he had left behind. Quietly collecting his suit and the keys to his car, he set out on his long drive home in the dark. *At least taking the normal way back will give me plenty of time to get this whole mess sorted out.*

THIRTY-ONE

Not What I Meant

CHARLIE'S THOUGHTS rolled in an angry jumble, the night around him feeding his mood. Gripping the wheel tightly before striking it with a fist, he grimaced; "How can this be happening?" he whined aloud to the empty interior.

"Don't take it personally," a deep voice replied.

"Dante!" Charlie shouted in surprise, his eyes darting around to look in the space behind him before his cohort appeared in the passenger seat next to him.

Chuckling, the newcomer teased, "You know how long it's been since I rode in a car?"

"No idea," Charlie focused on the headlights ahead of him, his shoulders slightly hunched in disgust. The white stripe flashing past almost hypnotic, he heaved an exhausted sigh. "Why would Karma let this happen?" he finally demanded.

Dante had been waiting patiently, ready to help the younger man when he was ready. "Karma doesn't really have anything to do with this."

"The hell she doesn't!" Charlie bit back. "She let Brett have Tabs, an' now Phil gets my mom? How messed up is that?"

"Who says Phil gets your mom?"

Gripping the wheel with rage, Charlie ground his teeth, in no mood for games. "He was there; he's gonna date her. That's more than should be allowed!" Making the turn onto the dirt road that served as Purgatory's private drive, he growled, "I'm gonna figure out how to stop it."

"Charlie, you wanted your mother to be looked after," Dante pushed, the darkness around them growing deeper on the empty stretch of desert that surrounds their headquarters.

Stomping on the breaks, the car slid to a stop and Charlie leapt out, slamming the light metal door with a bang. Running his fingers through his hair, he seethed. Tilting his head back, he stared at the clear sky above them; millions of twinkling lights decorating the black canvas. "Tha's not what I meant," he stated when Dante joined him. His companion climbed onto the hood of his car and waited without a reply.

Turning to face him, Charlied sighed, "Yeah, I wanted her t' be ok without me, but Phil?" A sick thought seeped into his mind. "She didn' earn all that on her own, did she. Phil's been medalin' in her life for a while," he considered aloud. "Is that why Karma sent me t' see her? To announce their official beginning?"

"I don't know," Dante denied quietly. "You'd have to ask Karma or Phil about that, but I doubt either of them would admit it, even if it were true."

His brow furrowed, Charlie demanded bitterly, "What are you doin' here, anyways? You should be in bed asleep right now!" He turned away, staring into the distance. Able to make out the faint outline of their compound, he sighed.

"I tagged along," Dante informed him evenly. "I wasn't invited, but I was a little curious about your mother."

"Bull shit," Charlie didn't look at him. "Nothing happens with the Forgotten Angels that isn' planned or assigned somehow. Why was Karma havin' me followed?" When only silence surrounded him, he turned around to find the hood vacated. "Well, tha's jus' great," he mumbled.

Staring at the car, he no longer felt like driving it. With a wave of his hand for focus, he transported the vehicle, placing it next to Karma's Ferrari under the long covering that ran along the back of her haven.

Arriving in the kitchen, he opened the fridge and helped himself to a glass of Phil's milk.

Moving to the transparent wall next to the cacti, he stared out at the dark sky. His anger dissipating, he sipped his drink. His eyes grew distant as he considered Keeper, Karma and the rest, as he had only grown more curious about them since arriving there. With the vastness of the universe, he wondered again where the powers that be had come from.

"There," Karma's voice soft, she moved next to him. Raising her hand, her shimmering red gown flowed down her arm and surrounded her body in waves of shiny silk. Her finger indicating a patch of light in the distance, she left the exact location vague.

"I thought you were gonna stay out o' my head," he stated dejectedly.

"I don't need to read your mind to know what you are thinking," her laughter tinkled lightly. "I know you're upset. Dante told me."

"Yeah, like you weren't watchin' the whole thing," he polished off the beverage and disposed of the cup with a flick of his wrist.

"Oh, baby," she sighed. "Don't be angry. Phil's done an excellent job of taking care of Bethany. He will be a good mate for her. Did you really think she would remain alone forever?"

"No," he sighed. "But I wouldn'a chosen him, either."

Her gaze fixed on the location she had indicated in the cluster of stars, she exhaled loudly. "Charlie, listen to me. Phil serves his purpose, but he doesn't have the stomach for what lays ahead of us. It's better that he be used on such tasks; like seeing to your mother. I know that she's important to you. That's why I have provided for her."

"What about Tabs?" he bit angrily. "Were you providing for her, too?"

Cutting her eyes over at him, Karma's jaw grew tight. "I have a good deal of patience," she informed him, "and you are wearing it thin."

"Oh yeah?" he gave a surly reply, "Then why don' you jus' tell me what's goin' on an' stop with all the cloak an' dagger business?" Meeting her gaze with an furious glare, he demanded, "Haven' I been a good servant? Always done what you asked? When do I get some real trust around here?"

Her eyes narrowed, their usual mahogany growing lighter. "I'm not sure you're ready."

"Oh, I'm ready," he half grinned, his voice taunting her. "You want me on your side so damn bad, you better do some explaining," he threatened.

Taken aback by his boldness, her mouth fell open and formed a small *oh* before she replied, "Don't get cocky, Charlie. You are indeed a great asset, but you have much to learn before we're ready to make our move."

"Now you're talkin'," he grinned in earnest. "You said I had passed my final test, I thought that meant I was like graduated or somethin'," he teased.

"No, hun," she still appeared tense. "You were ready to begin taking assignments, but there is still much for you to learn. You must be much stronger and in control before…" her voice trailed away.

"Before," he rolled his finger in the air, indicating for her to continue. "Don' leave me hangin'," he cajoled, a true feeling of serenity settling over him. "Karma, I chose to stay here. T' be your minion an' do your bidding. You can tell me the truth."

"The truth is an ugly thing, Charlie," she straightened her small frame and stepped back. Turning to the atrium, she glided away from him, "I'm not sure you can handle the truth; at least not yet."

Following her to the new set of windows, he could feel his anger rising once more. "You're a real bitch," he shouted at her back. Unable to stop himself, he sent a wave of energy slamming into her, knocking her forward a step before she spun around to face him.

Her eyes bright green, her features appeared contorted in a mixture of pain and rage. "You dare attack me?" she shrieked.

Horror shot through him, the realization of his existence slapping him firmly. "I didn' mean it like that," he stammered, dropping to his knees before her. "I jus' want you t' trust me," he begged.

Moving to stand before him, her eyes danced with green flames of rage. "Trust you," she hissed, her fingers trembling as she reached for him. Her digits digging through his hair, she found his scalp and instantly transported him to the darkness of her quarters.

THIRTY-TWO

Kings and Kingdoms

CHARLIE REMAINED ON THE FLOOR, her hands pressing against his skull. Breathing in deep, heavy pants, he opened himself to her. Fear gripped his chest and his heart pounded, sending loud pulses of blood through his ears. "Karma," he whispered.

"Shh," she instructed, adjusting her grip on him. Scouring his thoughts, she riffled through everything, even more deeply than she had done a few weeks ago when he had opened himself to her. Finally satisfied, she closed his mind and stepped away. "You are quite taken with Clarisse. I had hoped that having her would satiate your desire, and you would grow bored with her."

Blinking up at her drawn features, Charlie swallowed hard, causing his Adam's apple to move up and down beneath his taught flesh. "I love her," he finally stated, unable to elaborate beyond that simple explanation.

"Yes, you are deeply connected to her. I see now that it is useless to think you will ever willingly let her go," she stated quietly, turning her back on him. Telepathically igniting the candles, she bathed the room in a soft glow.

"Please don't take her from me," he begged in a hoarse whisper. "I'll do anything... whatever you want."

"I know that you will." One by one, she opened seven of the sets of curtains that protected her viewing screens. "I've never told you about my windows," her voice shifted, picking up a lighter tone. Glancing at him over her shoulder, she stated crisply, "Get off your knees, Charlie. Join me, and let us discuss kings and kingdoms in earnest."

"Kings an' kingdoms," he repeated as he got to his feet.

"Yes, the rulers of vast empires," she indicated a scene flashing before them on the first monitor.

Watching the dirty, fur covered lot, he observed, "I don' think this is modern."

"It isn't," she agreed. "This is how this world looked when we first came here."

Inhaling deeply, his chest rose and fell in a heavy sigh. "Thousands of years ago," he stated flatly.

"Yes, several millennia. We were a group of travelers and settled here to watch them grow. In time, Keeper and I took on the role of guardians." Taking a step to her right, she indicated the next screen, and he followed, watching a horse drawn carriage rolling over what hardly qualified as a road. A group of marauders rode into the scene, attacking the entourage. "Eventually, we created our children and set the magical plane as a firm division between their world and ours. Dividing this place that we might share it without discovery."

Charlie stiffened, the hairs on the back of his neck prickling him. "I still don' understand why you would care about us," he admitted.

"You don't have to understand. All you have to do is believe," she turned to the next wall, where the third device displayed bodies strewn along cobble-stone streets. "When we were discovered, I purged the knowledge from the earth, setting things right again."

His jaw clenched, his pulse thumped in his neck, but he remained silent. On the fourth viewer, battles raged, and he could see men fighting against one another, over and over. Pursing his lips, he turned the next corner to find that time had moved forward, with their weapons and clothing changed, but the blood and death remained.

On the sixth window, an angry mob appeared before him, and he watched a flag being burned. "This is recent," he nodded at the demonstrators, certain the gun-wielding figures were inhabitants of the middle east. "Like, very close t' today."

"Yes, this is only a few decades ago. And things have grown more violent since," she said softly. "These men have grand ambitions and desire to have this entire planet under their boots. They are but the latest to harbor such desires, with ideas that would destroy this world if allowed to fester."

His palms sweaty, Charlie rubbed his fingers across them anxiously. "What are you gonna do about them?" he whispered.

"I've already done it," she replied. "Things are in motion and all that is left is to prepare." She turned away, leaving him to stand alone before the mayhem. Moving to one of the sofas, she sank down onto the fluffy cushion. Stretching out upon it, she looked up at the ceiling above her. Watching the light of the candles flicker, she sighed, "I've grown tired, Charlie. Over and over, we've played out this cycle."

Having moved to the last of the exposed windows, he stared at the familiar landscape; a scene that had been famous even before tragedy struck it. Not able to draw his eyes away, he watched as a jet crashed into a building, the rock in the pit of his gut growing heavier. He had been in grade school when it happened and recalled the feeling of fear the event had stirred within him.

"They deserve to be punished," he agreed through gritted teeth. "You're going to, aren't you... like those guys we blew up," he thought of the war-mongers he and Dante had dealt with on their first mission together.

Not giving him a reply, Karma closed her eyes. Sliding the curtain over the window, Charlie had seen enough. Glancing at the eighth and final curtain, the one she had failed to reveal, he wondered for an instant what that screen would divulge.

Turning to her, he observed her prone figure, her round curves accentuated by the red silken dress that hung about her and draped over the front of the sofa. The back of her hand resting against her forehead, her pose reminded him of paintings he had seen of medieval damsels in distress.

"I'll help you do this," he stated more firmly. "Give me a job an' I'll see that it's done." Peeking at him with one deep brown orb, her face remained expressionless. He stepped towards her, taken with the idea of connecting with her intimately. He had not done so since Clarisse had joined their household, but he could feel the pull of her on his spirit.

Offering her his hand, he took her warm fingers in his. Massaging them lightly with his thumb, he tugged firmly, guiding her to her feet. Several inches shorter than him, she looked up at him, her clear honey colored eyes piercing his. Raising his left hand, he ran his fingers through her deep brown locks, the streaks of red tantalizing his digits as they searched for the firm flesh hidden beneath. Pushing his way to the back of her head and the nape of her neck, he caressed her affectionately.

"Charlie," her bright red lips beckoned to him.

"I'm here," he replied, pulling at her being as she had done to him on many occasions. Separating them from their bodies, their spirits mingled as a million points of light dancing around them. Holding her in place, their bodies pressed together firmly, their flesh grew numb and distant, as if it no longer existed.

"*Charlie*," her voice lilted again, more forcefully, but he had gone too far to be dissuaded. The light exploded around them, flooding the space as their souls were melded into a single entity, complete with no beginning or end between them. Free of his earthly trappings, he mingled and danced with her spirit. His wife, his mother, and the world that surrounded them all slipped into oblivion.

THIRTY-THREE

Legacy

CHARLIE AWOKE on Karma's bed, his clothing wrinkled and in disarray about his stiff frame. "What the hell," he mumbled to himself as he tried to sit up before sinking back into the pliable surface; *shit*.

Resting for a moment, he tried to swallow, but his mouth felt dry. *What the hell were you thinking?* he admonished himself in the dim light. Mentally searching the room, he found nothing and confirmed that he was alone. Transporting himself to one of the bathrooms, he selected a stall and stripped himself for a cold shower.

Allowing the water to pummel the top of his head, he leaned against the wall. Guilt ate at his gut, despite his belief that sharing himself with their benefactor wasn't really cheating. Somehow, he doubted that Clarisse would feel the same way. Cutting off the spray, he summoned a towel and pressed it to his face.

"I can't tell her," he said aloud. Inside his chest, his heart raced at the thought of doing so. However, making his lover angry came in second to the thought of hurting her. Her clear blue eyes filled with pain would destroy him. His mind made up, he would keep the secret if he could, and vowed he would never allow it to happen again.

Transporting to his room with the cloth around his waist, Charlie pawed through his drawers in search of clothing. Kari's dark eyes watched for a few minutes before he asked, "You ok, mate?"

Startled by his presence, Charlie jumped slightly, but did not turn to face him. "Yeah," he offered with a shrug, "I've got a lot on my mind. I had dinner with my mom last night…"

Swinging his feet to the floor, the other man stood, relieved at the reason for his roommate's demeanor, "How's she doing?"

"She's doing great," Charlie chuckled, "jus' great. Phil's been keeping her company."

"Phil!" Kari coughed, "You say he is with her?"

"Yeah," Charlie's brown hair dripped as he nodded. "Karma set them up together. He's going to be looking after her, I guess."

"Oh," Kari's lips formed a perfect circle as he considered the situation. "It's for the best then, mate," he reassured his friend.

"Yeah, I'm sure it is," Charlie selected a shirt and jeans before he disappeared. Arriving on their private beach, he donned the clothes and sank down to sit on the side of the raised platform, where their bed stood empty behind him. His heart ached, the idea of Phil taking his father's place more than he could stand. A moment later, he sensed Clarisse's presence and drew a deep breath before shifting into her plane of being. "Good morning, love," he managed with a tiny smile.

Her crystal blue eyes rimmed with red, he could tell she had been crying. A stab of pain shot through his heart, but he held his tongue and allowed her to open the conversation before he admitted to anything. "What's the matter, baby?" he asked after she gave no reply to his greeting.

"What will happen to us?" she asked in a soft voice.

"I dunno," he shook his head, running his fingers through the waves and drying his hair instantly. "Karma's got so many schemes, it's hard t' keep up with where we fit in th' picture."

Clarisse's hands flew to her hips in the form of fists. "You were with her," she voiced her suspicions tightly. "Last night. I know you came home from vising Bethany, but you weren't here, and you weren't in your bed." The only place he could have been was the one place she had only seen once and would never visit again.

"Yeah," he sighed, not bothering to deny it. "I stayed in her haven. She showed me more about how an' why they're here, an' I slept there. I'm sorry it made you worry," he offered the apology and hoped it would suffice.

Inhaling a ragged breath, she accused, "You would choose her over me."

"No!" he shouted, twisting to face her squarely, "I would never choose *anyone* over you."

Staring into his deep brown orbs, Clarisse searched for the truth. He had sworn to her many times that he loved her, but she had her doubts. "Why would you stay with her, then?"

"Because," he blinked but didn't look away, "It's not like that. Bein' connected t' her isn't the same as making love to you. I can't explain how or why; it's not sex, Clarisse. I swear to you, it's not the same."

Chewing her lip anxiously, she caught a hair that floated on the breeze and smoothed it. "I believe you, Charlie. I know that where Karma and magic are concerned, things are far more different and difficult to define." Stepping forward to sit beside him, she buried her toes in the sand. "I'm ok with it, if you have to…" her voice trailed away.

"I won't do it again; I swear it," he huffed. "I would never do anything t' hurt you."

"Don't promise me that," her voice quivered. "I'd rather not have a promise you can't keep standing between us."

Staring at her, he ran his tongue over his teeth. "You think I'd break my word?"

"I think it will happen again. Karma wants you, Charlie. I've felt it when we are together, at the house," her brow furrowed. "I think someday she will get rid of me so that she can have you for herself."

"No," he shifted to face the ocean. Watching the waves glide onto the shore, he elaborated, "She knows that I would do anything t' keep you. She has allowed me t' have you, an' you are her power over me."

"What's that supposed to mean?" she gasped.

"It means, she's gonna use us against each other, baby," he lifted his arm and dropped it over her shoulders. Drawing her firmly against him, he sighed, "Whatever Karma's legacy may be, rest assured that you an' me are meant t' be a part of it."

"You're saying we will do what she wants," she snuggled into him, her hand pressed against his chest. Rubbing him through his cotton tee, she caressed the muscles beneath it. "Can you live with that choice? I know that Dante spoke of crossing her."

"Yeah, but if he does, he'll do it without us," he placed his free hand over hers. "I don' feel right about making plans behind her back, even if I don' agree with everything that she does."

"Then I guess we will hold each other while we can and hope for the best," Clarisse agreed.

Watching the couple on her office screen, Karma leaned forward and placed her elbows on her desk. Smiling, she felt relieved that her most prized minion remained tightly in her grasp. "Our circle is almost complete," she informed them, knowing they could not hear. "When our house is full, we will be ready, and you will both serve me to the end," she promised them, a small giggle of delight escaping her lips at the thought of what would soon come.

About the Author

Anyone who knows me could tell you, I am a friendly kind of person, never met a stranger and take up conversations anywhere at any time. I work hard, and my mind never seems to shut down, as I wake up often in the middle of the night with ideas pouring out and demanding to be dealt with. Of course that means much of my books were written in the middle of the night.

I grew up and still live in the great state of Texas where everything is bigger, where we have warm weather and a central location. I love my state, my town, and my family, which includes my four sons, my significant other, and many friends as well.

I have thoroughly enjoyed writing this story and hope that you will love reading it just as much. And of course, there will be many more adventures to come.

You can follow Samantha Jacobey at:
    Website: www.SamJacobey.com
    Facebook: https://www.facebook.com/SamJacobey
    Twitter: https://twitter.com/SamJacobey
    Pinterest: http://www.pinterest.com/samanthajacobey/

Also by SAMANTHA JACOBEY

https://www.lavishpublishing.com/authors/samantha-jacobey/

A New Life Series – an epic adventure, TORI FARRELL's life IS one wild story... escaped from a biker gang and running from drug lords... used by the FBI and hoping to protect her present from her past... IT'S DARK - IT'S BRUTAL, and it's WORTH EVERY MINUTE OF IT!! (Mature read, 18+ for graphic sexual content and violence, including rape)

Summer Spirit Series - no one EVER had a summer romance like this… Charlie visits another plane, parallel to our own, where Summer Angels and Dark Angels battle over the fate of man. A unique twist on an old idea that will keep you guessing; will Charlie and Clarisse ever find their HEA? (New adult)

Irrevocable Series – Armageddon through the eyes of an entitled seventeen-year- old, BAILEY DEWITT's life has become a broken mess... after her parents died unexpectedly, she didn't think it could get any worse. But when the arrogance of man catches up and puts the entire world into a dooms-day spiral, there will be only one place she can run to - the one place she wanted desperately to escape. Can she and Caleb build a life together when the world is falling apart? (New Adult)

Teach Me to Prey – in this standalone thriller, JASON TRUITT and his friends have gotten their way for years. Deceit, sex, and foul play aren't normally covered in the curriculum, but they're doing whatever it takes to get under BECKY STEWART's skin. When one of the boys turns up dead, it's a race against time to save the others; a STUNNING STORY that will get your heart racing and leave you breathless by the end… (New Adult)

The Wicked Awakened – a Halloween novel; a five-hundred-year-old witch wants to turn SARAH MATTHEWS' body into her new home… A twisted tale involving a coven hell bent on seeing that she succeeds. Who will come out on top in this epic battle of wills? (Mature read, 18+ for graphic sexual content and violence)

The Binding - One cursed diary will change two strangers forever...Can Meri and Rider use her mother's old book to figure out why someone is after them? Or will the guilty party succeed, ripping the tome away before killing them and then slithering back into the darkness... (New Adult)

Sweet Christmas Series - Life isn't always sweet, even for girls called Candy. Candice Parker's life has never been easy. Plagued by losses and setbacks, each day is a struggle for the petite brunette and her young son. When fireman Gary enters her world, he is one mistake she refuses to make; but after tragedy strikes, she may not have a choice. (New Adult)

Also from the Lavish Publishing family

Love on the Double Duo
L.A. Remenicky
https://www.lavishpublishing.com/authors/l-a-remenicky/

The Monroe brothers fall fast, they fall hard, and they fall forever. But the road to true love isn't always easy.

Loving Jessie's Girl – Book 1: Until AJ Monroe left Indiana after college he had always lived in his identical twin brother's shadow. He had made a life for himself in Denver, Colorado, away from Jessie, away from Indiana. But when AJ feared for his brother's safety, he left everything behind to step back into the shadow he thought he had outgrown. Finding his brother was AJ's only concern...until he met Jessie's girl.

Fiercely independent, Rina Abbot hid her true situation from everyone, including her best friend, Jessie. Out of money and unable to care for her rescue dogs she had no choice but to accept the help of the handsome stranger with a familiar face. Afraid to trust him, she tried to ignore the feelings he stirred within her as they searched for his missing brother.

But secrets never stay secrets for long.

Finally open about their feelings for each other, Rina's secrets began to wreak havoc on their lives. Would Rina's secrets force AJ to give up his dream of loving Jessie's girl?

Beyond Duty – Book 2: After serving in the Marine Corps, Jessie Monroe has finally found a life beyond war. He's focused on being an EMT and helping his best friend rescue dogs, until he happens upon a curvy blonde stranded with a flat tire and no jack.

On the run from her past, Dori Graham is slow to trust any man, and she tries to ignore the spark of interest she feels for her handsome savior, but a friendship grows between them.

When Dori's past invades her new life, Jessie vows to rescue her. Saving her will take him beyond duty and into his own personal hell. Calling upon his training as a Marine and the depth of his feelings for Dori, Jessie will need the mental strength to battle to save her and, ultimately, save himself.

When Dori's past invades her new life, Jessie vows to rescue her. Saving her will take him beyond duty and into his own personal hell. Calling upon his training as a Marine and the depth of his feelings for Dori, Jessie will need the mental strength to battle to save her and, ultimately, save himself.

www.ingramcontent.com/pod-product-compliance
Lightning Source LLC
Chambersburg PA
CBHW060220180626
46813CB00007B/2896